the KIDS AREN'T all right

EMILEE KING

ISBN-10: 1966173045
ISBN-13: 978-1966173045

To Nan:
because you threatened to kill me
if I harmed your favorite character.
I did this for you, brother.

Keep your head, kid. You're gonna be all right.

"Peter!" Leslie shouted, lacing up her black high tops in a rush. "Get down here! You're going to make us late again!" Her fingers were going so fast that one lace got pulled too hard, effectively ruining the knot.

Leslie huffed as she pulled the laces apart and started over, taking the time to go through what Dad had taught her so many years ago, almost out of habit, though she'd rather die than admit she still remembered it.

Loop the ear, wrap it around, pull the other ear and whoop dee do, baby cakes, you've got a bunny rabbit. Now we better tie that little guy up. Wouldn't want to lose our rabbit, would we?

Satisfied, she tied the other shoe and slung her marker-ridden backpack over her shoulder as she straightened up. "Pete—"

"Chill," Peter said as he jumped down the last two stairs and slid into the kitchen, loose papers spilling out of his open backpack and his sandy blond hair still wet from the shower he decided to take five minutes ago. "I'm here." He dashed into the dining room to grab his prized golden letterman jacket where he left it after breakfast, his shoes squeaking against the hardwood floor, then he headed for the garage. "Come on, let's go."

Leslie rolled her eyes and followed. Their five-car garage was stuffy, the Arizona heat already warming up the place despite the early hour. Two of their four vehicles were missing—Mom and Dad had both left for work. The beat up vehicle in the back corner was a junker Dad and Uncle Hayden were working on together. Peter walked up to the yellow car in front of them and shoved his backpack in the passenger seat, sliding inside just as Leslie jumped in the backseat. The garage went up and they were finally on their way to school.

Peter was a scary driver. Leslie didn't know what he had to do to bribe the Driver's Ed teacher to give him a license, but heavy Benjamins must have been involved. She strapped her seatbelt on then braced her arms against her window and the front seat in an effort to keep from sliding around everywhere.

Leslie had her own driver's license, but Mom said she wouldn't get another car until the big seventeenth birthday—for now, Leslie had to share with Peter. Which meant Leslie too often turned to a squashed bug on the back windshield, forgotten.

Amid fearing for her life, her phone buzzed. She took it out of her pocket to find a text from Amanda.

'Happy Hump Day, Les. I'll buy you lunch today to celebrate.'

Leslie scoffed to herself, Peter's radio blaring in the background, as her fingers typed back. *'What notes do you need today, pea brain?'*

Immediate buzz. She must've already been at school.

'You got me. Just bio, lit and algebra. And if you want to do my art project, I'll add dessert. It's supposed to illustrate rebirth or something weird like that.'

'I'm not even in algebra. And you've had three weeks to do that project.'

'Right. Maybe you could come down from your calculus kingdom and help a girl out.'

Leslie sighed but didn't get to respond before Peter slammed on his brakes, making Leslie shoot forward and nearly miss hitting her head on the front seat. Prepared to protest at the stop—they were so going to be late—she paused when she realized where they were. It was Hump Day, which meant it was Wednesday, which meant it wasn't Tuesday or Thursday. And that meant Peter picked up his girlfriend.

Kill me now.

Megan Reed came out of her gorgeous white mansion carrying a small purple floral purse (which Leslie never understood. It's school. You need a freaking notebook) and her black drill team bag, her name bedazzled in rhinestones glinting in the sun.

"Hey, baby," she said as she slid in the passenger seat, throwing her bags down at her feet, and gave Peter a brilliant smile. Her raven wavy hair was pulled into a ponytail, her bright pink tank top accenting her perfectly tan arms—literally perfect. Not a tan line in sight.

Is she even human?

"Hey," Peter said, and Leslie could hear the stupid grin in his voice before Megan leaned over and kissed it off.

Leslie's phone buzzed again, and she was grateful Amanda provided a distraction from the train wreck in front of her. *'r u coming? I can't do Fingernail Boy without you.'*

'It's Wednesday so we had to stop in Make Out City.'

'What a puke bowl.'

'Tell me about it.'

"Can't you do this during Chemistry or something?" Leslie complained, setting her phone in her lap. "I've got a Bio test first period."

Peter started driving before his face had cleared Megan's, and for twenty harrowing seconds sped blindly down the street before Megan finally pulled away. Sitting back in her seat, she gave Leslie her standard greeting glare.

"Leslie."

"Megan," Leslie responded, matching her curt tone. Then she went back to her phone, tuning out the conversation in the front.

'Queen B has been picked up. Successfully on my way.'

Again, Amanda responded right away. *'You could always ride with me, Les. Skip the love sessions.'*

'Yeah no thanks.'

Peter was terrifying behind the wheel, but he couldn't top Amanda, whose driving without a license combined with crappy car that could die any second made you want to write your last will before she put the thing in drive.

Amanda sent a face with its tongue sticking out. *'Your loss.'*

Mercifully, Peter pulled the car into the school parking lot and parked in his usual stall: the bottom right corner, as far from the front doors of the school as possible. The entire football team parked in that corner; it's where they hung out when sluffing class.

The whole team, practically, was already there, standing around or sitting on hoods of cars with their girlfriends, all in their golden letterman jackets. Leslie snuck out of the car and walked as fast as she could toward the school before anyone could really notice her. Except Clive. She waved back to him. Clive was the quarterback, the smartest, nicest, and most descent of them all, in Leslie's opinion. Clive was sweet and respectful of Leslie, and never ignored her or made her feel like trash. The rest of the team though—including Peter's best buds Duane and Jamal and Tank—were a bunch of 'A' words Mom didn't like her to say.

She made her way through the parking lot as fast as she could without running—the morning sun on her back was already starting to make her sweat through her community art class t-shirt. A small smile spread on her face when she caught sight of Amanda's blue beater parked in the third row, with a cracked right mirror and missing fender. It was easy to spot among the sea of shiny jeeps, slug bugs and convertibles.

There were too many people still left in the common room; the warning bell had rung but students still stood around in denial, administrators trying to usher them to class. Leslie weaved expertly through the throng to room 105B, sliding into her seat next to Amanda in the far left corner when the final bell rang.

"Cutting it close, don't you think?" Amanda whispered with a grin, tapping her newly manicured fingernails against the obsidian science table.

Leslie started digging through her overflowing pencil bag. "I made it before the bell, didn't I?"

"I was betting you'd be late. Guess I owe myself five bucks."

Mr. LaRue cleared his throat, somewhat gaining the attention of the class. "Good morning, students. I hope you've all prepared well for your exam today. We'll begin once roll is taken."

He then began going through each person's name, his voice monotone as though he'd rather be anywhere else. It was October now—a few months into the school year—but he still acted like it was the first day. He never tried to learn anyone's name or seemed to even really look at their faces, addressing students by the color of their shirt if he called on anyone.

"So, any testing tidbits of wisdom you want to give me today?" Amanda whispered, striking up their usual roll-taking conversation since they were both at the end of the list. Her shoulder length light brown hair was done up in a fancy braid, her makeup applied, gold bracelets lining up and down her arms. She told Leslie they were the latest fashion trend—anyone who was anyone was wearing them. As with all of Amanda's fashion advice, Leslie didn't care.

"Study it," Leslie whispered back. "Or pay attention. Your call."

"Quick, quiz me."

"Okay…" Leslie flipped through the vocabulary words in her head. "What's an ecosystem?"

Amanda bit her glossed lip as she thought. "That's with the money problems, right?"

Leslie stared at her for a second. "No, that's the economy. This is biology." She shook her head. "Did you even read anything out of the textbook?"

Amanda smirked. "Not a page." Rather than be bothered by that fact, she pointed a not-so-subtle thumb to the kid in high waist khakis sitting next to her. "He's starting early today."

Sure enough, Fingernail Boy was picking off his fingernails, then breaking them into tiny pieces and arranging them on the table in front of him in some elaborate pattern.

"Amanda Webster," Mr. LaRue droned.

Amanda raised her hand, giving it a cute little flick that Mr. LaRue didn't see. "Here."

"And lastly, Leslie Wyman."

"Here," Leslie called.

Mr. LaRue picked up a stack of tests and began passing them out. "As always, use a sharpened number two pencil—nothing mechanical. We are all traditional here. No cell phones, pagers, laptops, MP3 players, watches or anything else technological. No talking. No cheating." He stopped in front of Amanda, breaking out of his monotone speech to give her a look. "And eyes on your own paper."

Amanda bit the inside corners of her mouth, what she did to keep herself from smiling, and nodded seriously. "Yes, sir. No problem."

Once Mr. LaRue had moved on to the next row, Leslie slid an extra pencil to Amanda, who gave a quick nod of gratitude. She liked to pretend she didn't care about education—therefore not owning a pencil— rather than admit that she struggled with learning and couldn't afford the supplies. Leslie tutored her, allowed for minimal cheating, and supplied things when needed, but there was only so much she could do when Amanda decided not to put in the effort.

School came naturally to Leslie—plus she'd spent two hours studying last night. She finished the fifty-five questions in twenty-seven minutes, while it took the majority of the class about an hour. Amanda was still struggling through the last few questions when Mr. LaRue gave the five-minute warning.

Leslie spent her extra time doodling in her sketchbook. She never did any actual drawings in class; the thought of someone peeking over her shoulder made her nervous. So she just drew shape after shape, swirl after swirl, shading certain parts in to make flowers or optical illusions. It made the hour and a half go by much faster.

"That was impossible!" Amanda complained once the bell had rung and they were safely down the hall. "How does LaRude expect us to know all of that?"

"He teaches it to us," Leslie said flatly. Sometimes Amanda's excessive complaining got on her nerves. "He tells you what you need to know and then you learn it."

Amanda shrugged. "Whatever."

They made their way to Government, a class that would be of at least some interest, maybe, if Ms. Knudsen didn't teach it. A self-proclaimed feminist in all the wrong ways, she spent the hour and a half bashing the male gender as a whole, somehow managing to teach the government system while pinning all the defects of it on the men it's run by. The essay prompts she gave were ridiculous, but all Leslie had to do was watch Peter and his cronies for a half hour and she had plenty of material on the flaws of a male-based society.

But the worst part about Ms. Knudsen wasn't her teaching style or blatant sexism despite claiming to fight for equality—it was her almost fanatic appreciation for the most successful and renowned prosecutor in the state.

"All right, class," she started, adjusting her black blazer jacket as she stepped out from behind her obsessively organized desk. "As always, we'll start out today by getting an update on Arizona's highest profile case." She pulled down the screen—still barely able to reach up and grab the string despite her four-inch black heels—then turned on the projector and played a news clip, basically just restating the information they'd known since the school year started.

Julian Zambrano. Short, stocky and Italian. A giant spider web tattoo on his giant bicep. A glare that could probably kill someone if they sneezed the wrong way. Notorious murderer, gang leader, drug dealer and money launderer. The worst of the worst Arizona had to offer. Police had finally apprehended him awhile back and the trial was supposed to start within the next few weeks. It was going to be a long and nasty one, but officials weren't worried despite all of Zambrano's connections because they had a superstar on their team.

Leslie ducked her head when she heard the achingly familiar voice come on over the cheap speakers, promising they would give the criminal the incarceration he deserved. That was the word she used. 'Incarceration.'

How formal.

The sound of the screen going up filled the silence, then Ms. Knudsen clapped her hands together. Leslie tried to duck her head farther down, her nose nearly squished by her desk, but Ms. Knudsen zeroed in on her anyway. Like every other day.

"Leslie?" she asked, her voice innocent as though she did not understand the awfulness that stained what she was doing.

Leslie popped her head up and tried to act casual rather than like she was hiding. "Yeah."

Ms. Knudsen smiled in excitement, practically bouncing on her heels. "Do you have any insider information you could share with us? Any wise words from your mom?"

Leslie didn't know why her teacher got so excited, since the same answer was always given regardless of the truth. She hoped her face didn't look red, though her voice squeaked slightly, when she told the whole class, "No, I don't."

Ms. Knudsen deflated (had she really been expecting anything else?) and got on with her lesson. It took Leslie about three minutes before the heat completely receded from her face and she could breathe normally again.

Despite facing it literally everywhere she went, yanking herself out of Mom's encompassing shadow was harder at school. Leslie didn't know why. Maybe it was the way Ms. Knudsen looked at her, like Leslie would suddenly sprout the famous Raelyn Wyman and Ms. Knudsen would get to swoon all over her. Or maybe it was the way everyone at school tended to remember her only as Mrs. Wyman's daughter rather than Leslie. And that made a lot of people try to be Leslie's friend for all the wrong reasons, like the Wymans' deep pockets or extensive contacts. Or, until the lovely Megan came along and clearly staked her turf, to get to Peter.

Never for just Leslie. And that drove Leslie insane. If she could somehow black out her last name from all her identification, life would be a ton easier.

Half fuming and half embarrassed from the whole thing, Leslie spent the rest of the period doodling in her sketchbook. Afterwards, she separated from Amanda for Calculus, but met up with her in the hallway later so they could head to lunch together.

"What'll it be today, Les?" she asked as she swung her wallet on its mini strap around her finger. "Cheese covered cardboard, mystery meat, or expired mixed vegetables?"

Leslie sighed at her options, watching the line ahead of them as it moved. "Probably cardboard."

After going through the line, Leslie carrying her tray of pizza and Amanda her wilted salad, they made their way through the chaotic lunchroom to the table on the edge of the throng where Chet was sitting.

Chet was a big guy. Average height, rounder build, long ratty black hair pulled into a mini bun to match the black stubble on his face, a blue bandana always tied around his forehead, beefy hands stained spotty black. He was the guy you thought was turning thirty years old, not a senior in high school, and pretty much everyone—even the macho football players—made sure to scramble out of his way.

"Hey Chet," Leslie said as she plopped down next to him, stuffing her backpack under her plastic gold seat.

Chet glanced up to give them a grin with his small mouth. "Leslie. Amanda. Nice to see you." He'd already finished his tofu vegan nastiness and was working on writing in his notebook with his favorite fountain pen, creating flawless cursive. Probably writing more poetry. "How has this fine fall day been for the two of you?"

"Oh, you know," Amanda responded, dumping the container of ranch dressing all over her salad. "Failed a Bio test, watched a lame video with a man dressed as Benjamin Franklin in Government, then played Bejeweled through Algebra." She grinned before using her fingers to shove lettuce in her mouth. "It's been your average Wednesday."

Chet winced at Amanda's lack of manners, but Leslie had gotten used to it. Amanda just didn't use utensils. Ever. For as long as they could remember. Leslie tried eating that way once when she was ten.

"Leslie," Mom had said before the first bite of mashed potato could reach little Leslie's mouth. "We aren't animals. Use your fork please."

"But Mom," Leslie had whined. "Amanda eats like that. Why can't I?" She was too young to understand the politics of it all, why comparing herself to any of the Websters' habits would doom the finger eating regardless of what Mom actually thought about it.

"Did Ms. Knudsen call you out again?" Chet asked, his voice cast in sympathy.

"Yeah," Leslie muttered in between bites of pizza. "I don't even get it. Like why? What's the point when she knows I'll just say no and nobody cares anyway? It's so ridiculous. I hate it."

Chet nodded. "I imagine so. How is your mom doing with the case, if you don't mind me asking?"

Leslie shrugged. "Same as always. Maybe more stressed out, since Zambrano's a big one, but she can't ever let that show in public. The real chaos will start when the trial begins. She'll be in Phoenix for weeks at a time." She took another bite of tasteless pizza. "My dad has big corporate meetings at the dealership in the next couple weeks, which means Peter will probably claim leadership and my house will be overtaken by blockheads." She gave a wry grin. What a glamorous life Mrs. Wyman's daughter lived.

"My place is always available, should you need it," Chet offered. "My mom would love to have you as a guest."

"I'll keep that in mind."

Once Amanda had cleaned off her ranch hands, Leslie took out her notes so Amanda could at least pretend to look over them. Then she took out her sketchbook and continued working on her next art assignment, which was just a short list of ideas. The theme was "love in death" and they were only allowed to use charcoal. So far, Leslie hadn't come up with anything good. Instead, she started sketching a frame around her few ideas.

"Have you heard back about the art competition?" Chet asked after a minute.

Leslie shook her head without looking up from her work. "Not yet. But I expect I will any day." She couldn't think too much about it or she'd break out in a nervous sweat.

Chet was all encouraging. "I'm sure you'll place. You're a marvelous artist."

The bell screamed over the buzz of talking students. Chet immediately packed up his notebook and pen, and stood, filling the space around him and causing three freshmen standing behind him to back away. "I'll see you two ladies later."

Both Leslie and Amanda gave a distracted wave. "Bye Chet," Leslie called. After a few more lines in her sketchbook, she packed up and yanked an unwilling Amanda to English Literature.

After school, Leslie was faced with a difficult choice: finding a ride home. Amanda went straight to work at Ready Dawn Day Spa and Chet met with an animal rights group. Leslie's two options were to ride the school bus alone or go find Peter before football practice and beg for the keys. Both were miserable and sure to cause a lot of unnecessary pain, and—though she would never ever admit it—scared her like crazy.

Steps slow and hesitant, Leslie made her way down to the football field on the other side of the school. Sure enough, Peter and the team were hanging out on the bleachers, several of them gathered and daring each other to jump down a certain number of rows while the others watched.

These guys are complete idiots.

Leslie took a breath to calm herself (why did they freak her out so much anyway?) then made her way through the chain link door and onto the field. Thankfully Peter was sitting on the edge of the bleachers, Megan practically in his lap as they cheered on the losers jumping off the bleachers. Megan's skanky friend Tasha—also Jamal's girlfriend—saw Leslie first, and smirked.

"What's up, loser?" she scorned, her smiling lips way too big for her pinched face. "Nice t-shirt."

Leslie ignored her. Peter's face fell into annoyance when he turned and saw her, and Megan rolled her eyes.

"What do you want, Les?" Peter asked, keeping his voice low as if afraid someone would connect him to her. Like they hadn't been related since birth.

You're so pathetic, Peter.

Refusing to be unnerved, Leslie just held out her hand, palm up. "Keys."

Peter scoffed. "You wish."

"I have to get home. Don't be dense."

"Take the bus." He turned back to his friends, completely apathetic to whether Leslie lived or died in the slaughterhouse that was the school bus.

"The bus already left." Wasn't completely true, but it would be by the time she got back over there.

Megan clicked her tongue in mocking disappointment. "Too bad."

That made the back of Leslie's neck burn, and not from the sun. She cleared her throat, nervously glancing at the players who were starting to notice her. "Peter, just give me the keys."

He didn't even turn his head, making his answer barely audible. "Not a chance, Les. Get lost."

Leslie hesitated. "If I don't show up at home, Mom will wonder what happened."

"Mom won't be home until tonight," Peter answered, picking an irritating time to start paying attention to Mom's schedule. "Besides, she'd probably be excited if you never showed up ever. Less headaches."

Infuriated, Leslie turned and stalked away, folding her arms tight across her chest when she heard Peter, Megan and various others burst into laughter behind her.

I hate you all.

She was concentrating so hard on her angry steps, she almost ran right into Clive. Mortification spread from the back of her neck across her face.

"Oh, uh, excuse me," she muttered, tapping her fingers together. "That was…um, yeah."

Clive just grinned, football bag slung around his shoulder, perfect white teeth illuminating against his chocolate skin. "Hey, no problem at all, sweetie." He took one look at her and understanding crossed his face. He nodded behind her. "Your brother giving you a hard time?"

"Uh, well…" She brushed her hair behind her ear, giving a glance behind her shoulder. "No more than usual."

Clive leaned forward and lowered his voice. "I was the last one outta the locker room. Peter left his backpack on the floor by his locker. Keys are inside." He straightened up and winked at her. "But you didn't hear it from me, eh sweetie?"

Leslie gave a small grin and nodded. "Right."

Clive smiled again and patted her on the shoulder. "Later Leslie." Then he stepped around her, jogging up to his team.

Following the tip, Leslie snuck into the locker room—empty, just like Clive said—and found Peter's mess of a backpack. Thirty seconds of digging and she had the golden lanyard with the keys.

Way to go, Clive.

The parking lot was half empty when she got to Peter's yellow car. She couldn't wipe the smile off her face as she slid in the driver's seat, having to scoot it up a bit to reach the pedals, and drove out of the parking lot to her house.

The Wyman's house was beautiful—as an artist, Leslie had to admit the perfect balance between modern and regal. Big windows with elegant drapes peeking into the front room, towering archway and four concrete steps leading up to the front door, with a stone lion statue standing under the doorbell. The lion had a crack on the side of its face from the time seven years ago when Peter knocked it over.

He's always ruining everything.

The best part about football season? Peter didn't get home to eat all the good food before Leslie got the chance. Opening their double pantry door, Leslie scoured the filled shelves until she found the bakery croissants and last bag of barbeque chips (take that, Peter) then dug through the fridge to find the leftover chicken salad from last night. There weren't any spoons left, probably since Peter never brought dishes back from his room, so using an oversized serving fork would have to work.

Knowing Mom wasn't home, Leslie kicked off her shoes in the middle of the kitchen and flung her backpack on the island counter, sitting up on the tall iron chair to dig into her lunch, scrolling through social media feeds on her phone as she ate. Once she'd been through everything, she just sat and listened. It was quiet. Leslie liked it that way. When the big house was full—like with Mom's work meetings or Dad's dinner parties or Peter's football cronies—sounds vibrated off of every surface, bouncing off the marble floors and wide windows and chandelier fixtures, making it insufferably loud. But when it was empty, you could feel the stillness, crisp and soft at the same time. It was one of the only good parts of living there.

She sat for a minute in peaceful silence, noticing how the light from the ceiling hit the China bowl on the counter, creating a perfect prism of color. Her finger traced the granite, mimicking paint brushstrokes and imagining how she could possibly get that same magically lifelike quality of color in her pieces. After making a few notes in her sketchbook, she moved on to homework.

One thing Leslie appreciated about her house was all the comfortable places to sit. There were couches in the living room, front room, sitting room, Peter's room (ew), the loft, the office and the covered deck. So when Leslie pulled out The Great Gatsby to read for English Lit homework, she had plenty of options as to where she could relax and read. It was still too hot for Leslie's taste to be outside, so she ended up sprawled on the white leather sofa in the sitting room, swaying her arm back and forth over the edge so her fingertips brushed against the hard floor.

After a few hours of reading, Leslie realized football practice was almost over—Peter would find out what she did. And Leslie did not want to be home alone when he came back. Grabbing an apple from the counter, she paused to consider the color: deep shiny red, like a model's lipstick or a newly blossomed rose or a freshly caught lobster. None of those things could be incorporated well with her 'love in death' project, except maybe the rose, and the only other red thing that came to mind that could match the theme was blood.

Blood and death. Not really two of her favorite things.

Shrugging, Leslie shook the thought out of her head, got back in the car and headed for the dealership.

Stan's Auto Mart was the most successful family-owned car dealership and repair shop in the country. It had humble beginnings, since Dad had started it on his own with Uncle Hayden in their garage when Leslie was five, but it had completely exploded over the last eleven years. Now they had three buildings in Arizona, one in New Mexico, one in Utah, and they were in talks with the Vegas area. Dad mostly ran the business side of it now, which was why he always kept a car in the garage to work on in his limited spare time.

"Reminds me of the glory days, baby cakes," he'd say when Leslie would find him working in the garage after midnight. "It's always good to remember where you came from."

Leslie parked in the back of the massive glass building in Peter's employee parking spot. He didn't work much during the football season, but nobody would think it was weird to find his bright yellow car there. The security guard—Mr. Dufrane—was a crazy stickler on parking tickets.

Styles, the receptionist with too much pep who drank too much tea, waved from across the main floor, per usual, and Leslie gave a halfhearted wave back. Before Leslie could be offered any disgusting herbal liquid or killed with enthusiastic fake friendliness, she headed up the back stairs to the offices, passing by the cubicles and popping her head into the first office to find Dad's lanky younger brother typing away on his triple monitor.

"Hey, Uncle Hayden," she greeted, giving a quick wave.

Uncle Hayden's face spread out into a huge smile. "Les-lie! How's my favorite niece doing today?"

Leslie gave a small grin and shrugged. "Pretty good, I guess."

"You checkin' in on your old man?"

"Yep."

Uncle Hayden nodded. "Well do me a favor and have a good one, all right?" Then he clapped and reached into the full apothecary jar next to the framed picture of him and his girlfriend. "Watermelon, right?"

"It's the best of the best."

He tossed a watermelon Jolly Rancher at her, and she had to step forward to catch it. Then she gave another wave. "As you were."

"Roger that," he called after her as she left, popping the candy in her mouth from her one relative she wasn't ashamed to be related to.

Dad's office was almost as big as their living room at home, and it was the playroom Mom didn't let him have. The far wall was glass, looking out over the entire front of the dealership, and his desk took up that side. The other half of the room was filled with two couches, a foosball table, a Ping-Pong table, with two flat screen TVs on the walls and a treadmill tucked in the corner next to a table full of food and a stocked mini fridge that was open to all customers. Dad excelled at business because he put business second. Friendship always came first.

His phone rang right when Leslie walked in, and he held up a finger to her as he answered. "Stan Wyman, what can I do for you?" He was wearing his favorite light blue button up shirt with the sleeves rolled up, so it must've been a good day. Leslie went and sat on the corner of his desk, aimlessly kicking her legs in the air and watching the people out the window, pondering how she would paint the details of their faces from this distant image.

"What are you up to, baby cakes?" Dad asked after finishing his call. "How did education go today?"

Leslie shrugged. "As good as any other day." She thought for a moment. "I took a Biology test today. Pretty sure I aced it."

He clapped his hands together, his grin making his balding head seem rounder. "That's my girl! Did Hayden already reward you?"

Leslie stuck out her tongue to show the shrinking candy. He nodded and sat down in his big leather chair, getting absorbed into his colossal single computer monitor.

"How's work?" Leslie asked, grabbing a yellow sticky note and pen from his desk organizer.

"It's been good, baby cakes," he said, distracted, as he clicked his mouse. Leslie took a mental picture of him just like that, eyes wider, leaning forward with chin in his hand, engrossed in the screen. Then she started doodling a cartoon version on the sticky note.

"How's the art coming?" he asked without breaking away from the computer.

Leslie gave a small grin. She loved that question. Dad was the only one who ever really asked it. He was nice enough to at least pretend he cared about her art—his interest was more for her sake than anything, nothing compared to the personal eternal stake he had in Peter's football. The favoritism used to drive Leslie crazy, but she'd learned to take what she could get.

She didn't look up from her drawing, not letting her hand stop as she spoke. "It's good. I got a new project in honors, but I don't know what to do. The inspiration river has run dry."

"Hm," Dad muttered. "What's it about?"

"The theme is 'love in death' and I have absolutely no ideas. I don't want to do some sappy star-crossed lovers thing, you know? No girl bleeding out while she confesses her love to the boy with her last words."

"Not really your thing, huh."

"No, not really."

"You'll think of something, baby cakes. You always do." Now he was typing on the keyboard. His ability to half multitask astounded Leslie. Probably had to pick it up after marrying Mom. "Have you heard about the art competition thing yet?"

Leslie's skin prickled at the thought. Dad was the only one she'd told about her entry, besides Amanda and Chet of course. She wanted to place *so* badly she almost couldn't stand it.

"No, but I probably will soon. I think."

"Hm."

They worked in silence for a bit. Once Leslie finished her cartoon sketch, she peeled it off the desk and held it up proudly.

Dad's face lit up, taking it from her. "Hey, now, look at that. That's great, Les." He rolled his desk chair away from her to the wall, sticking the drawing next to the fifty or so others that Leslie had done throughout the years, some of the worn ones dating back to when she was six.

Right then, Peter walked in with a green Jolly Rancher sticking out of his mouth, his hair plastered to his sweaty face, still wearing his workout outfit. He ran here.

Leslie rolled her eyes. *What a showoff. His arrogance never ends.*

"There's my superstar!" Dad exclaimed, picking up an autographed football from its stand on his desk and throwing it. Peter caught it reflexively with a grin and tossed it back. "How're the boys looking? You ready for the game on Friday?"

Peter ignored Leslie, walking up to the desk and leaning his muscular arms on it. "Yeah, it's lookin' good. Coach says we'll blow it out of the water. Not even worried. Championship here we come."

Even with the somewhat close proximity, it took a moment for the destructive wave to hit her.

"You smell disgusting," Leslie said, wrinkling her nose. "It's called deodorant."

Peter smirked. "It's called actually doing something with my life." He raised his arms mockingly and took a step toward her. "Want a hug?"

Leslie jumped up from the desk and backed away. "Heck no, creep. You're so gross." Last time he caught her unprepared, and Leslie swore it fried her nose. She couldn't smell normally for at least a day after.

"No offense, Peter, but it's true," Dad said. "You're going to stink up my office. Les, give him a ride home so he can shower. And tell your mom I'll be home for dinner. Just finishing up a few things."

"Got it," Leslie said, already fast walking out the door.

Peter jumped in front of her and pushed her back, holding out his hand with a glare. "Keys."

She scoffed. "You wish."

"Les." He pushed her again. "Now."

Leslie pushed him right back. "No, you bonehead."

"Hey!" Dad called with an edge to his voice. "Not in here, you two. Leslie drove here so she drives home. Go now."

Leslie gave a smug smile to a silently protesting Peter and walked out, getting the keys out of her pocket and swinging them on her finger.

She already had the car started when Peter reluctantly got in the passenger side, slamming his door harder than necessary. Leslie couldn't keep the smile off her face as she reached up and pressed the door of the small roof compartment, opening up to Peter's prized sunglasses, and put them on.

Peter did a double take when she turned her head to back out. "What are you doing? Take those off."

Leslie shrugged, delivering his usual line as they exited the parking lot. "Driver's in charge."

"Not kidding, Les. Take them off."

"No."

"Now."

"No."

He reached over and tried to take them off her face, almost making her swerve into the wrong lane, but she hit his hand away. "Jeez, Peter, I'm driving! Chill."

Peter breathed a loud sigh of annoyance, then rolled down his window all the way. Leslie hated that. She tried to roll it up, but he held the button down on his side. Once she gave up, he turned the stereo up all the way, the rap music Leslie couldn't stand threatening to blow out her eardrums.

"Turn it down!" she shouted over the music and flapping wind.

"Can't hear you!" he shouted back, tapping his fingers against the outside of the car to the heavy beat.

Leslie gritted her teeth. What horrible, awful thing she had done to get him as an older brother, she would never know.

After announcing their arrival to the neighborhood, Peter finally turned the music down. He was still relaxed from the windy ride, but his voice was harder.

"Don't ever take my keys again."

"Don't ever try to strand me at the school again."

Peter shook his head. "You're so immature. If you want people to treat you like an adult, then you have to act like one. Figure out your own ride."

"Immature?" Leslie snorted. "That's rich, coming from you."

"You're so stupid."

"Where do you think I learned that from?"

Leslie pulled into the garage, turned the car off, then threw both the glasses and keys at Peter before getting out and going inside the house.

Mom was already home, chopping up vegetables at the counter. Her dark blonde hair was still up in an elaborate bun, showcasing her diamond earrings, and an apron guarded her tan blazer and skirt. She'd shed her heels though. Mom always cooked barefoot, even in the dead of winter.

"Les, could you help me for a minute?" she asked when Leslie came in. Leslie decided a long time ago that the best way to describe Mom's voice was rubber cement: it spread on smooth like a dream, but if you let it harden, good luck ripping your craft apart. To this day, Dad still said Mom sweet-talked him into marriage.

"Yeah, sure."

"Wash your hands," Mom instructed even though Leslie had already started for the sink. Peter came sauntering in, bringing his stench with him, and Mom held out a hand to stop him before he left. "Please shower before dinner, all right? Quickly."

Peter nodded. "I'm on my way."

"First, sweetie, can you get this platter for me?" she asked. "I can't quite reach it."

Peter retrieved the platter for Mom, then went off to relieve us all of his awful smell. Mom slid a cutting board to Leslie and handed her tomatoes and a knife. "Cut these for me, then mix up the salad. I just have to finish the meatloaf and we'll be ready."

Leslie went to work, knowing that if her cutting job made dinner late, she'd never hear the end of it. Family dinner was at six every night. You couldn't miss it. Even on the weekend you'd have to get special permission to be gone.

It was something Leslie never understood. Mom was insanely busy. She had the best excuse of anyone to just order pizza or get takeout every night and let everyone eat when or where they wanted. But no. As much as possible, she bent her schedule around a cooked family dinner in the dining room. Both Leslie and Peter had made their cases for Chinese in their rooms—one of the few times they ever agreed—but Mom had shut that right down. Dining room and meatloaf won.

"How was school?" Mom asked as she stirred her mashed potatoes.

Leslie shrugged. "It was fine."

"You had a test today, didn't you?"

"Yeah. Biology."

Mom nodded like she remembered, even though Leslie was pretty sure she hadn't told her what test it was. "How was it?"

"Good, I guess. Just a test."

She finished with the mashed potatoes just as Leslie finished the salad. Mom looked over the greens to approve it.

"Can you set the table?" she asked, wiping her hands on her apron. "We'll be ready once your dad gets here."

Leslie grabbed a stack of plates, forks, knives, napkins and cups, and made her way to the dining room. Their oak dining table could sit up to fifteen people once all the pieces were in, but most times it was just a square—Mom and Dad at each head, Peter and Leslie on the sides. The chandelier hanging from the ceiling sent sparkles everywhere, and the sun shone through the two big windows, glinting off the surface of their backyard pool.

The garage sounded. Dad was home. Leslie quickly finished the set up just as Mom came in carrying a platter of meatloaf. Dad followed her with the potatoes and salad, going back to the kitchen while muttering something about serving utensils. Mom spread out the food as Leslie filled the cups with ice and water.

"Where's our son?" Dad asked when he came back in with the salad tongs.

"Shower," Mom and Leslie answered at the same time.

"Ah." Dad nodded and gave a grin to Leslie, making her grin too. "Better for all of us then."

Peter came rushing in right after, just as everyone was sitting down, and Leslie had to bite back a scoff. Leave it to Peter to show up at the right time. No work but all the reward.

They all sat down in their spots and waited for Mom to say grace. Mom had her own version of praying over the meal, and Leslie didn't realize it was weird until she got older and saw other people do it. Mom had everyone put their hands in their lap and close their eyes, then she repeated the same thing every time: "We are grateful for this meal and the strength it gives us. We are grateful for this house and the protection it provides for us. We are grateful for each other and the love they give us. We are grateful for life and the opportunities it has given us. We are blessed."

Then everyone is expected to open their eyes and repeat at the same time: "We are blessed."

And then Peter snatches the bowl of mashed potatoes or the pretzel salad or whatever he considers to be the best thing on the table. Mom stopped telling him to slow down a long time ago. Leslie reached for her mixed salad and began dishing up.

"How was work today, Rae?" Dad asked, politely waiting for Peter to finish taking basically half the meatloaf.

Mom gave a tinkling laugh. "Busy as always. The office was a mess—Monique had her babies today."

"You don't say," Dad said, passing Leslie the basket of bakery bread, the only thing on the table that Mom didn't make.

"We were in the middle of a meeting and her water broke." Mom said the words with excited fondness, even though Leslie thought the whole ordeal sounded gross and embarrassing. "She was rushed to the hospital and had the twins within the hour." She gave a soft sigh. "Isn't that amazing?"

Both Peter and Leslie were chowing down on their food as their parents talked. Leslie had learned over the years to at least pay half attention to the conversation because she never knew when she'd be called on. Mom didn't like them to be distracted during dinnertime. She didn't even answer her phone unless it was an absolute emergency.

"Well, we should send her something," Dad said before a bite of meatloaf.

Mom nodded, daintily stabbing some salad with her fork. "I sent flowers to the hospital, but I'll give her a better package once she gets home. Diapers are expensive these days." She straightened up then, as if pulling herself out of her thoughts, and glanced at Peter. "Peter, I heard about Leslie's test but haven't heard anything about your day."

Yeah, Peter. Tell her how you were daring your buddies to jump off the bleachers and not crack their heads open.

"A college scout came to talk to us at practice today," Peter said, his big mouth full of an even bigger piece of meatloaf. Mom cleared her throat, and he swallowed before talking again. "Talked to us about recruiting. Said there's going to be Arizona State scouts at the game on Friday."

"All right!" Dad crowed. "Did you tell 'em you're the best linebacker they could hope to get?"

Peter nodded with an excited grin. He thrived off of unnecessary praise. "Guy said they'd watch us seniors most and take notes. Anyone who catches their eye will get a one-on-one meeting with a scout to talk about options."

"Well, that's wonderful, Peter," Mom congratulated warmly. "You've worked hard to make this last season your best. You deserve the attention you're receiving."

Leslie had to look down at her plate to keep from rolling her eyes. *Does he really, though?*

The rest of the dinner conversation was taken up by Dad, who told a verbatim story of the sale he made today by inviting the customer up to his office for a rousing game of foosball. Then dinner was over; Leslie and Peter were always on clean up duty, each job specifically assigned since they used to fight incessantly over who had to do what. Peter unloaded the dishwasher and Leslie loaded it. Leslie washed the extra dishes and Peter dried them. Every night. There was a mini whiteboard inside the cupboard above the sink that kept track of how many days they'd done the dishes without fighting. The current record was three.

Dishes were part of their chores that went toward their allowance. Contrary to popular belief, Leslie couldn't just buy whatever she wanted. Mom and Dad didn't spoil their kids despite their fat wallets; they told them to work for what they wanted. So Leslie and Peter got jobs and did chores for a decent allowance. Although Leslie's biggest source of income was often Peter himself—he bought her silence when she caught him sneaking out or discovered Megan had stayed after curfew. Little sister to an airheaded jock was the business to be in these days.

Leslie anticipated some kind of counterattack, since Peter was probably still fuming about the whole 'stealing his keys' thing, but Mom lingered in the kitchen, wiping off the counters, so Peter behaved.

The second they were done, Peter bolted for his room upstairs. Leslie was about to follow suit, but Mom's voice stopped her.

"Les, can I talk to you for a moment?"

Oh great. Leslie took a quiet breath to gather strength, then turned to face Mom, who'd taken off her apron and was sitting on a chair at the island counter. She pulled out the chair next to her and patted it. Leslie sat and waited.

Mom sat with her legs and arms crossed, still looking as formal as ever. "Have you given any more thought to college, Les?"

Leslie couldn't trap the mini groan that came. They'd already had this fight, but since Leslie was only a junior in high school with two years before turning eighteen, she guessed they'd have this fight many more times before she'd get out.

"Now don't give me an attitude," Mom said with a slight sharpness to her tone. "It was just a question."

Nothing is ever just a question with you.

A small, tight knot started forming in Leslie's chest, but she just shrugged. "A little, probably. I don't know. Why?"

"I feel it's time to start planning for you. A bright future is ahead, and I want to make sure you're prepared and have everything in place."

That was such an innocent answer, but that was because it was her standard speech.

Leslie shrugged again. "I probably will plan it then. When I know what I want."

Mom's job relied on her not giving anything away in her face. Nothing showed now. "Sweetie, you do know. You're going to go to college and get yourself a solid education. Everything starts there." She smoothed out her perfect skirt. "Now, I'm thinking you should apply to Dartmouth, Yale, Harvard, Brown, and Princeton to start. Once we get responses we can work from there. You need to decide what degree you want to receive and how far you want to go. Now, I think you—”

“Whoa, stop,” Leslie said, her mind reeling at the blows Mom delivered so flippantly. “I don’t…*Dartmouth*? I…I don’t—”

“You’re smart, Leslie,” Mom reassured, completely misreading Leslie’s distress. “You’re modest with me, but I see your report cards. I talk to your teachers. You have what it takes, I know you do.”

The knot was tighter now. Leslie had to take an extra breath. “I don’t want that.”

Mom didn’t break her neutral expression. “What do you mean you don’t want that?”

Leslie gritted her teeth in frustration. “You know exactly what I mean. I don’t want to go. I don’t want to do that.”

“Do what?” Mom demanded, more sharpness seeping in. “Get a valuable and respectable education?”

“No, I just…I don’t want to go to those places. I want to focus on…on something else.” Her palms were getting sweaty. She rubbed them against her denim shorts, but it didn’t help.

“Something else? What is more important than education, Leslie?”

Leslie had to stop and think since words were starting to jumble in her head. “I’m still going to go to school, Mom, but nothing like Dartmouth.” Her mouth got dry at the thought of telling Mom this for the first time ever. “I’m going to go to one with a…program. For art. An art program.”

"Art?" Mom repeated in surprise. "I didn't realize you were that serious about it. I thought it was just a hobby."

No, Mom, it's only my favorite thing in the world to do. Or were you too wrapped up in football to notice?

"I'm completely serious about it. That's what I'm going to do. I'll find a small college out of state that has a good program and go from there."

"Oh, but…" She gave a fake mini laugh. "You can't…there's no future in that. Do you understand that? You can do it on the side, to be sure, but the likelihood of getting real success through art is—"

"I don't care about likelihoods." Leslie's heart was pumping now, and it hurt next to the growing knot in her chest. "And I don't care about your opinion. I'm doing what *I* want because it's *my* life. Not yours."

That crossed the first line. "Leslie Ann Wyman do not talk to me like that. You will apply to those schools." Mom's tone was absolute, her posture still perfect despite the emotion of the situation, as if they were in the courtroom rather than their kitchen.

Leslie hated that. She hated feeling like she was just another one of Mom's clients in need of being put away. Put in their place, their place that Mom deemed was right.

"No, I'm not!" Leslie half shouted. "Stop trying to control my life!" Then she jumped up from her chair, stomped up the stairs, ran into her bedroom and slammed the door shut.

Her room was big, but Leslie did her best to make it feel smaller. She got big furniture. She had a giant king-sized bed with cast iron posts, plus a big desk, a dresser, a double bookshelf, and two beanbags. The walls were filled with drawings and paintings and printouts, some of them hers and others ones she'd found that gave her inspiration.

Leslie fell onto the purple beanbag, buried her face in it, and screamed. She was so angry she couldn't stand it. She knew that. But anger and frustration didn't match the tight knot in her chest.

That happened sometimes. There were just certain topics or situations or things that made Leslie lock up. She knew that since she was a kid and learned to just accept it. It had become a radar for her, in a way, because when she got that knot in her chest, she knew she was heading into scary waters.

Leslie stayed sprawled on her beanbag for the rest of the evening, waiting for the knot to go away. It never did.

~~~

"Welcome to Up Your Allie, how can I help you?" Leslie asked the middle-aged lady hanging onto three bouncing kids that were standing on the other side of the desk.

"We're here to bowl," the lady said with a smile. "Two games for the four of us, please."

Leslie tried to smile back as she typed on the cash register. She didn't like kids, but she couldn't avoid them working at a bowling alley. "All right, that'll be forty-five fifty."

The lady paid with a credit card, and Leslie got them each their shoes and set up their lane, pointing to where they could get their bowling balls. Then she went back to the desk. The bowling alley was always a certain level of busy in the afternoons and evenings
~~~

because it was one of the only places to go for fun in the town of Malquetta, Arizona. Most of what Malquetta had to offer was fancy business parks. The pool had closed for the year, making the movie theater and bowling alley the only places for people to hang out unless they wanted to leave town.

Unfortunately, that meant Leslie frequently ran into people she didn't want to see, like people who went to her high school. They were here now. Peter, Megan, Jamal, Duane, Tasha, and a group of others. Peter and Leslie had ignored each other, per usual, which she was just fine with. The less interaction the better.

Leslie went over to the other side of the alley to clean up the arcade a bit, grimacing through the sticky knobs and chewed gum stuck underneath seats. She wasn't supposed to work alone, but she did often, since her coworker Vanna spent nearly her whole shift smoking out back.

Giving up on the arcade, she went back to the front desk, adjusting the collar on the black polo she hated so much. "Up Your Allie" was written across it in big white lettering. They used to be called "Up Your Alley" since that actually made sense, but apparently there was already a bowling alley with that name in Wyoming and they actually sued. To avoid any complications, the owner changed the name after his sister Alexandria. Leslie thought the whole thing was senseless, and the shirt was even worse. But it's what made her money, so she dealt with it.

A twenty-something guy wearing a wrinkled brown polo and too big jeans sauntered up to the counter.

"What's up, Kenny?" Leslie asked him as she went through the change in the register.

He nodded at least five times, leaning up against the counter. "Good. Good. You good?"

"Yep. How's the bowling tonight?"

He pointed to a ten-year-old girl jumping up and down in excitement after bowling a strike. "She's pretty good. Pretty good shot."

"Yeah, that's cool."

Kenny nodded again, then walked back over to lane six. The employees always made sure to leave lane six open no matter how busy they were—that was Kenny's lane. Leslie had never learned exactly what disability Kenny had, but she didn't really care. Kenny was Kenny. And Kenny was hilarious. He hung out at the bowling alley all day every day, watching every game, applauding every strike, and offering constructive criticism for every gutter ball. Every few minutes you'd hear him shout "Good shot!" or "So close!" or "Gu-tter!" People in the community had gotten used to him, anticipated him, and several kids had become good friends with him. Kenny was probably Leslie's favorite part of the job.

"Hey!" a guy was calling from one of the tables. "Hey, can I get some service over here?"

Leslie didn't even look his way, since she recognized the voice and would take absolutely no part in that. But when the guy didn't stop yelling, she looked down the rows of bowling lanes and saw both of the kitchen employees were busy attending to other customers. And if the yelling caught the attention of the manager—Lee Chen—then Leslie would get busted for not helping out.

I hate my life.

Forcing her steps to be firm, Leslie made her way to the far table. The guy shouting—Peter's friend Duane—was sitting next to Peter. Nobody gave Leslie a second glance except Duane, not even Peter since he was too busy kissing Megan.

"What?" Leslie asked Duane flatly, glaring.

Duane looked her up and down a few moments, then grinned. "I'd like to order somethin' not on the menu, if you know what I mean." And the numbskull in the golden letterman jacket had the audacity to wink at her.

The terrible line caught the attention of his cohorts, causing them to turn and see what he was up to. Tasha and Megan snickered when they saw her, and the other guys howled with laughter, but Peter just did a double take and elbowed Duane in the ribs hard. "Chill, dude, that's my sister."

Duane's face went from teasing to surprised as he clutched his side. "*That's* your sister?"

Infuriated and mortified, Leslie turned and stalked away, around the front desk and into the office in the back. The knot in her chest was back, bigger than last night. She wiped her sweaty palms on her pants and tried to talk herself through her anger. They were all idiots. Leslie didn't care what any of them thought. She didn't care that Duane had been to her freaking house hundreds of times *and* talked to her—did he really not remember what she looked like? Was she really that invisible?

Doesn't matter. You don't answer to imbeciles like them. You don't need to bring yourself down to their level for approval. You don't care about them. You never have.

Leslie stayed sitting at the small table next to the fridge in the office until she heard the service bell ringing a hundred times in a row. Prepared to be annoyed, she hauled herself up and went back out to the front desk to find Amanda pretending to inspect the board of prices.

"Hello, there Miss," Amanda said, purposely chomping her gum obnoxiously. "Can I buy some bowling games or whatever?"

Leslie rolled her eyes but gave a small grin.

"You're so dumb."

Amanda went around the side of the desk and came through the divider, sitting in her usual chair set up by the cash register. Both Leslie and Amanda worked until closing, but Ready Dawn Day Spa closed at seven while Up Your Allie was open until ten. Since Amanda would result to cleaning asphalt before going home before she absolutely had to, she often stopped by to hang out while Leslie worked.

"So what should we do tomorrow?" she asked, scrolling through her phone absentmindedly. "It being Friday and all. What parties should we hit?"

Leslie took some bowling shoes people had returned to the desk and started putting them back in their place. "I think I'm gonna go to the football game."

Amanda stopped to stare at her. "Again? Didn't you go last weekend?"

"Yeah. So what?" she asked even though she knew it was weird because she hated football and—until last weekend—avoided contact with anything that had anything to do with it.

"Um, you've never gone in your life and now you want to go two weeks in a row." Her eyebrows furrowed. "You didn't lose a bet with Golden Boy, did you?"

Leslie shook her head. "Peter doesn't care whether I go or not. He probably doesn't want me to, actually." So imagine his surprise last Friday when he found out she was there. He still didn't care though. He just pretended he didn't know her.

"Um…okay." Amanda shrugged. "Whatever. You're a weirdo."

"And yet you're still my friend. So are you going to come with me?" Leslie hoped she would, since A. she didn't want to go by herself, and B. it was easier to keep Amanda in control on the weekends when not at a crazy party.

Amanda gave her a mischievous grin. "Sure. Unless, of course, I get a better offer."

Leslie rolled her eyes. "Yeah, whatever."

Leslie and Amanda didn't really date. It just wasn't their thing, for vastly different reasons. Technically, Leslie had a boyfriend. His name was Azz Williams (what his mother was thinking, Leslie had no clue) and he was nice. And friendly. And that's about it.

Really, by conventional standards, they were just friends. Amanda was the only one in the world that knew they hadn't even kissed yet—they'd held hands only once and that was because Leslie really thought he was going to throw up on the roller coaster. The only things they really had in common was their lack of desire to date the trash that populated their high school, and that they were sick of people asking about their love lives. Since they'd been friends since first grade, they made a pact halfway through freshman year that they were 'dating' and used each other as an excuse when needed.

So, no, Leslie didn't expect any dates on Fridays or Saturdays or any day. Amanda, on the other hand, was incapable of any relationship that lasted more than one night.

An explosion of laughter came from the far corner—Amanda turned toward it and Leslie wiped her hands on her shorts—then Amanda rolled her eyes.

"What a bunch of eggheads."

"You're telling me," Leslie agreed. "Duane tried to hit on me. And he didn't even remember who I was."

Amanda shook her head, her nose flaring. "What a jerk. You're better off though. If he can't recognize you then maybe his stupidity won't rub off on you."

Leslie mustered a tiny laugh. "Yeah, that's true."

The knot in her chest seemed to tighten when Peter's crowd finally walked out the front doors right before closing, and she waited for it to go away. It didn't. It seemed to last forever. Even by fourth period the next day, it hadn't completely dissipated. She just ignored it. At least, until the intercom came on, interrupting the class discussion on The Great Gatsby reading.

"Can you send Leslie Wyman to the front office, please?" the secretary asked over the speaker.

"Yes," Mrs. Fitz called, then nodded to Leslie. The knot doubled in size as Leslie stood and stiffly walked out with the entire class watching.

It's probably nothing, Leslie reasoned with herself as she went down the hallway. *It's probably something so trivial and lame and you're going to laugh at yourself for even being concerned.*

But Leslie was a good, smart kid, and good, smart kids only got called down to the office to get a candy bar for the 4.0 at the end of the semester, which wasn't for a couple weeks. *What could this possibly be about?*

Hesitantly, she opened the office glass door and went inside. Before she could get up to the front desk and ask what the whole thing was about, a freakishly tall lady with brown hair almost to her butt stopped her.

"Leslie!" she exclaimed, using one hand to grab Leslie's arm since the other was holding a big yellow envelope.

"Ms. Mac?" Leslie asked her art teacher in confusion. "You called me down here?"

Ms. Mac just nodded, gushing, and pushed the envelope at her. "I couldn't wait the whole weekend to tell you. Open it!"

Bewildered, Leslie took the envelope and opened it, pulling out a piece of stiff beige paper.

"You won!" Ms. Mac burst before Leslie could even read the paper. Then her eyes found the giant words on the center of the certificate: First Place. Leslie Wyman.

"You're kidding," Leslie breathed. Her eyes read the words over and over. First place. "I won the whole thing?"

"The whole thing!" Ms. Mac pumped her fists in the air like some bad cardio routine with no music. "*My* student won a district-wide contest because she is the bomb!"

"Wow." Leslie's face spread with a giant smile and she looked up from the certificate to a bouncing Ms. Mac. "That's crazy!"

Ms. Mac held up her hand and Leslie gave her a high five. "You deserve it, girl. You are so talented; it blows me away." She gave her a little push. "Bell's about to ring—go tell everyone how awesome you are!"

So ecstatic she thought she might explode, Leslie nodded and dashed back to class, reaching the door just as the bell rang and students came surging out. She waited outside until Amanda exited, dutifully carrying Leslie's backpack like all best friends should. Leslie yanked her aside in the hallway and held up the certificate before she could ask.

Amanda's eyes narrowed, then widened, and she screamed, causing a group of students to look their way, but neither of them cared.

"My best friend is Picasso!" Amanda yelled, jumping up and down, gold bracelets colliding, then she stopped. "Wait, his name was Picasso, right?"

Leslie just grinned. "Yes, it was."

"Awesome! We'll celebrate after the game, okay? Want me to pick you up?"

"You drive, I'll pay."

Amanda smiled. "And that is the solid foundation of a great friendship."

She had to go to work, so Leslie took her backpack and ran as fast as she could through the crowded school and to the far corner of the parking lot. Peter was just getting into the yellow car when Leslie threw herself in the backseat, barely registering Clive sitting in the front.

"Can you drop me off at Dad's work?" Leslie asked, breathless, before Peter had even gotten all the way in the car.

He was so put off by her excitement that he actually (accidently, probably) agreed. "Uh, yeah. I guess." He pulled out of the parking lot. "What's got you so worked up?"

Was Leslie still smiling? Had she ever smiled this much in her life? "I won! I actually, really, totally and completely won."

"Won what? The loser award?"

She didn't even take the jab; she just held up her prized certificate even though Peter was driving. Clive turned around and took it from her so he could read it.

A beautiful smile spread across his face. "Hey, now, first place!" He held up his fist and Leslie didn't even think twice about hitting her knuckles against his. "That's awesome, Leslie. Congrats."

Peter just rolled his eyes. "You mean you're so excited because they gave you a piece of paper for coloring on a different piece of paper?"

Leslie shook her head, taking the certificate back from Clive. "It's a big deal for culturally intelligent people."

"Right." Peter scoffed. "Whatever."

But for once Peter's cynicism couldn't put a damper on her excitement. She didn't even wait for the car to stop in the dealership parking lot before she jerked the door open and ran for the entrance.

"Uncle Hayden!" she yelled from down the hallway so when she skidded to a stop in his office, she would already have his attention. "Uncle Hayden, guess what?"

He was sitting as his desk, as always, and his face lit up when he saw her. "What's up, Les?"

She barely stopped to let herself take a breath. "I entered a district art competition and I won first place!"

His jaw dropped dramatically. "No way!"

She rushed forward and shoved the certificate at him, like he needed proof to believe her. His smile was wide as he looked it over, then handed it back to her.

"That's amazing, Les! I'm so proud of you!" He reached in his jar and grabbed a handful of Jolly Ranchers, then unzipped her backpack and dumped them in. She was off again with an uttered goodbye, running right into Dad's office.

He was on the phone. He smiled when he saw her, then held up a finger to her. She tapped her hand against his desk in agitation until he finally hung up.

Dad laughed. "What's going—"

"I won!" Leslie blurted, pushing the certificate in his face. "I totally won!"

"Now hold on there, baby cakes." His eyes focused as he read the document, then he gave her a giant hug. "Now that's my girl! Beating out the entire district. My daughter, the artist."

Leslie grinned. She loved the sound of that.

~~~

A door slammed. A moment of quiet. Then another slam. Stomping up the stairs, then a harder, louder slammed door, closer. Peter's room. Then a long set of quiet.

Leslie was sprawled out on her bed, face buried in her pillow, and she'd already changed into her pajama pants. It wasn't even eight yet, but she wished she could just go to sleep and forget today ever happened.

She turned her head to breathe, which was a mistake because she caught sight of the navy blue dress thrown in a wrinkled mess on the floor.

Oh, the dress.
~~~

It wasn't that Leslie hated being female, because she didn't. She just didn't really like anything overly feminine. No sandals. No pink. No makeup. And no dresses.

Leslie knew that meant she was weird, compared to most girls. Megan had told her more than once in very clear terms that she wasn't pretty at all, which was fine with Leslie because she didn't care to be. 'Pretty' was for other girls. Not Leslie.

But when Mom wanted to take the family to a lavish restaurant owned by one of Dad's new investors for dinner—to promote good relations, Dad explained—she insisted Leslie wear a new navy blue dress with a high lace collar that she just 'happened' to have in Leslie's size.

It made Leslie furious, but she hadn't really spoken to Mom since their college conversation last week and knew she was walking on thin ice. So she didn't argue, but she made a big hateful show about putting it on. And she kept her scornful remarks down to just three when Mom told her to at least put on a little mascara.

So in Leslie's defense, she was starting the night as the underdog, and it only got infinitely worse from there.

Really, it started with Peter (doesn't everything?) but Mom and Dad probably wouldn't remember that since Leslie's "negative attitude was affecting family time." Dad started talking about the last football game. Everyone was surprised to find that Leslie had gone— for the second week in a row, no less. That turned the conversation to what she did over the weekend, and Peter made the comment that she hung out with the two biggest losers in the school, calling Amanda a word that Mom did not approve of.

Leslie yelled at Peter, Peter yelled back, Dad yelled at Peter and Mom at Leslie and Leslie at Mom, and after the first fork was thrown Dad dragged his children out of there just so they could shout at each other the whole way home.

Needless to say, dinner was cut short.

Leslie often wondered if Mom ever wished she had different kids. Probably. Peter knew how to fake Golden Boy, but neither of them were anywhere near good enough to live up to the Wyman name.

Mom was a planner. She always had been, since day one, and Leslie could easily imagine little eight-year-old Rae in wedge heels carrying her notebook and bossing everyone around. Mom had her whole life planned out since she was probably eleven. Graduate high school early. Go to Cornell. Get married at twenty-one. Receive her degrees and become a prosecutor. First kid at twenty-five, then wait until she was twenty-eight to have the second—three was the magic number. Then she'd round it off with the third after she turned thirty-one.

That had been the plan. But one good date night and—boom—you've got an unwanted baby girl two years ahead of schedule. Add that to pregnancy complications that ultimately led to infertility, and Mom's life plan was completely blown up. No perfect family with three perfectly behaved kids spread three perfect years apart, who all said perfect things and smiled perfect smiles and studied at perfect schools and wore perfect dresses. Instead, she got Leslie and Peter.

What a disappointment.

Leslie gave a frustrated sigh into her pillow. Time was lulling and dragging and not going nearly fast enough. She went back and forth between staring at the ceiling and messing around on her phone. She thought about bringing out her sketchbook, but even drawing didn't sound appealing. That's when she knew it was bad.

Eventually her stomach made a loud grumbling noise. She hadn't eaten since breakfast—they were out of pizza at the cafeteria today and Leslie didn't take any chances on the mystery meat. The kitchen was a bad idea though: if someone heard the squeaky fridge open, it would all be over, and she'd hear yet again about how she ruined dinner. Didn't want to go there.

She sat up, remembering the bag of Cheetos and half package of powdered donuts in her backpack. Junk food would make the situation better. Then she slumped in resignation when she remembered she left her backpack in the office downstairs.

Dad had left. She knew that because he'd dropped them off at home, then sped away in fury. Peter was in his room where he would probably stay for the foreseeable future. Mom was probably taking a bath to calm herself down before Dad finally came back. Leslie's odds of not being seen were pretty good.

Turning the knob slowly, Leslie opened her door without a sound, then tiptoed down the darkened hallway (you can tell when Mom's angry because she doesn't turn lights on), making sure to avoid stepping on the second and eighth stair since those were the ones that creaked. Turn left at the stairs, head back through the mini hallway and into the first door on the right. It was that easy.

The light on the desk was on, but that was it, barely illuminating Leslie's backpack in the wood chair in the corner. Roughly twelve steps in and out, and Leslie was in the clear.

She got halfway when a soft voice stopped her.

"You're caught."

Leslie froze, turning to see Mom sitting on the floor behind the desk, a large box of old photos in front of her. She waited for the scolding to continue. Instead, Mom glanced down with a small smile on her face at the photo she was holding, gesturing for Leslie to come look.

Cautious in case this was a front for reprimanding, Leslie stepped around the polished wood desk and sat across from Mom, on the other side of the box. Mom held out the picture to her. It was the four of them—Mom, Dad, Peter and Leslie—in the hospital right after she was born, each parent holding a baby and beaming with pride.

"You were beautiful," Mom murmured, her voice like warm cotton. "You still are."

Leslie glanced at her, trying to gauge the situation. It was rare to see her like that: no makeup, frizzy hair in a loose bun, wearing black yoga pants and her favorite faded Cornell sweatshirt despite the hot weather.

"That was a long time ago," Leslie finally said because that was the only thing she could think of.

Mom just nodded, transfixed by the photo. "Sixteen years. Nearly seventeen."

Leslie was put off by her serenity. Was this a front? Was this some trick and as soon as Leslie got comfortable Mom was going to blow a gasket?

"So..." Leslie started, rubbing her finger against the side of the box. "Are you mad or what?"

Mom looked at the photo another moment before sighing softly and setting it back in the box, then glanced up to meet Leslie's eyes. "You're grounded. I hope you know that."

That made Leslie laugh once. "Yeah. Figured."

Mom let out a long breath. "Really, it depends on what shape your father is in when he gets home. He was rather angry. Rightly so."

Leslie thought of a hundred and one reasons why the whole situation wasn't fair—because really she shouldn't be in trouble at all—but decided now was not the time. The less she could keep Mom from yelling, the better.

"He told me about an art thing you did," Mom said out of nowhere. "He didn't get the chance to finish though. What was that?"

"Oh." Leslie hadn't told Mom about the whole art competition thing, just because she didn't know what kind of response she would get. Especially after the whole "I thought art was just a hobby" thing. "Um…well…"

Guess I don't have a choice now.

Leslie crawled on her knees over to her backpack, grabbed it, and crawled back. She hadn't taken the certificate out yet. She liked carrying it around with her—it brought her more happiness than anything else.

Gingerly, Leslie pulled out the certificate and handed it to Mom. She looked over it for a moment before her mouth turned up in a wondrous grin. "You won first place? Out of the entire district?"

Leslie was too nervous to speak, which was dumb, so she just nodded.

Mom glanced up at her. "That's amazing, sweetie. Wow. I knew you were good but I…" She smiled at the certificate again. "I had no idea. That's wonderful. Congratulations."

Well, that could've gone worse. Mom was in a very receptive mood, and it was rare Leslie felt like she could really actually talk to her without the words getting turned around.

Leslie fingered the side of the box a bit more. "Mom…about the whole college thing…I—"

The sound of Leslie's phone ringing cut her words off. She picked it up from her lap to see Amanda's face covered in fry sauce staring back at her, the number displayed across the screen. Leslie automatically glanced at Mom, who just nodded.

"Go ahead," she said, somehow settling back into herself, looking into the box again.

Leslie swiped her finger across the screen and brought the device to her ear. "Hey, what's—"

"Les!" Amanda blubbered into the phone. Crying. Amanda Webster was crying. "Les, I…I need your help…and…"

Leslie was so shocked by her distress that it took a moment for her to talk. Then her mind raced with possibilities. "What's wrong? What happened? Was it that guy you were with or…" Realization hit her. "Is it Naomi?"

Amanda's breath caught and she sobbed. "Yes. Les, I came home and she…she's on the couch like normal but she wouldn't…she wouldn't wake up and now…"

"Amanda?" Leslie tried to talk through the wall of crying, but Amanda was too frantic. "Amanda, listen to me. Amanda!" Finally, out of desperate fear more than anything, she looked at Mom and put her hand over her phone. "Mom, she's freaking out. She won't listen to me. What do I do?"

Mom's face got serious, and she reached for the phone. Leslie was suddenly overcome by so much panic that she just gave it to her.

"Amanda?" Mom asked, her voice smooth and calm and firm and relaxing all at the same time. "Amanda, honey, this is Raelyn. Leslie's mom. Can you hear me? I need you to calm down, okay? Can you do that for me?"

Leslie leaned forward as the knot in her chest, bigger than ever, came right back, tightening all her insides in such an uncomfortable way. But she didn't care. She just cared about Amanda.

"That's good," Mom complimented something Amanda said. "Can you tell me what's going on? Is it your mother?" Leslie could almost hear the hysterical answer on the other end. "Is she breathing?" Another muffled answer. Then Mom nodded. "Okay, sweetie, it's going to be all right. Listen to me, I need to you to put her in the car and drive her to the hospital, okay? You know where it is?" Pause. "Good. Leslie and I will meet you there. It's going to be just fine." Then she hung up, tossed the phone back to Leslie, and pulled herself to her feet, all in one movement.

"What's going on?" Leslie asked as she jumped up, even though she pretty much knew. "Are they okay?"

Mom was already out the door. "Go get in the car."

Leslie obeyed, grabbing her sneakers on the way, not realizing how hard her heart was pounding until she was belted in the passenger seat of Mom's silver car.

It only took a moment before Mom caught up. She threw her purse between them, started the car, and sped through the October night.

Leslie's fingers were numb as she laced up her shoes. She had to do each of them twice, and Mom didn't even tell her to get her feet off the dash.

Loop the ear, wrap it around, pull the other ear and whoop dee do, baby cakes, you've got a bunny rabbit. Now we better tie that little guy up. Wouldn't want to lose our rabbit, would we?

"Stay calm, okay Les?" Mom cautioned suddenly, eyes narrowed and focused on the road. "From what I gathered, it wasn't on purpose, but Amanda will need calm regardless. Can you do that?"

Leslie nodded. "Yeah."

They pulled up to Malquetta Community Hospital ten minutes later. Leslie let Mom lead the way through the emergency room doors; Mom went right up to the desk, but Leslie stopped when she saw a familiar figure curled on a chair in the waiting room. Steps hesitant, she made her way over and sat next to Amanda.

She glanced up when Leslie sat down. Her heavy mascara and eyeliner were smudged all around her eyes, like a soggy raccoon, and dried black tears stained her cheeks. She'd stopped crying but her breaths were still broken and ragged.

They sat next to each other in silence until Mom made her way over and sat on the other side of Amanda.

"They're taking care of her right now," Mom said, her voice hushed. "She's going to be okay. The doctors will let us know when she's awake again."

Amanda nodded without looking up from the ground. Leslie stayed quiet. It wasn't the first time Naomi had taken a toxic mix of pills with her alcohol—all by accident, she claimed—and it wasn't the first time Amanda had to take her to the hospital, but it was the first time Amanda had been that freaked out about it. And that freaked Leslie out.

Amanda's home life had sucked from day one, but Leslie didn't know for a long time. It took years for her to grasp why Amanda always came to her house, or stayed out all night with some guy just so she didn't have to go home, or started drinking alcohol so early, or why Mom wasn't very thrilled when Leslie came home one day from second grade and said her new best friend was Amanda Webster.

The Websters and Wymans weren't supposed to mix, but Leslie and Amanda didn't care. It just got awkward sometimes when the differences were capitalized. Like when Leslie worked three days a week at a bowling alley to supplement her allowance so she could have fun, while Amanda somehow worked full time hours while going to school and donated plasma so she could pay for the crappy single room apartment she and Naomi lived in.

Amanda had said so many times over the years she was just going to walk away. Naomi had never been a mother to her—Amanda had always called her 'Naomi' instead of 'Mom' even when she was a kid—and just ruined what little stability Amanda could create. Amanda never knew her dad, and there was another kid from another night, but he'd taken off a long time ago. He used to send a check every once in a while, but Amanda hadn't heard from him in years.

In short, Amanda didn't have a family. Naomi was addicted to so many things, Amanda had lost count. She just expected to come home every day and find her stoned on the couch. Often, she was unconscious. Amanda had been playing the game for so many years that she knew when it was serious enough to come to the hospital and when to just pour water over her and wait for it to wear off. In a moment of semi-drunken honesty, Amanda had once admitted to Leslie just how many times she came home to an emergency and considered letting Naomi die.

Leslie had offered her house multiple times over the years, even though they both knew Mom would probably veto that plan if they tried to actually make it happen. Mom had backed off and let Leslie and Amanda be friends—heaven knows how many times Leslie had pulled Amanda out of a bad situation, and she'd never been sucked in like Mom was afraid would happen—but everyone knew Mom still frowned upon the fact that they were besties.

It was hours of cramped chairs, TV buzzing in the background, coffee, and mumbled small talk. Amanda never said a word, but she did take a sip of coffee, which Leslie thought was an improvement.

Finally, a nurse in maroon scrubs came up to them. "Amanda?"

Amanda didn't even look up. She just set her cup of cooled coffee on the ground and stood, ready to follow the nurse to wherever Naomi was. She knew the drill.

Mom and Leslie followed a ways behind as the nurse led Amanda down a hallway and into a room. Amanda and the nurse went inside; Leslie and Mom waited in the hallway.

When the nurse opened to door to leave the room, Mom surprised Leslie by stepping inside. Bewildered, Leslie followed. Naomi Webster didn't exactly like Leslie, much less Mom, but Mom must've had some sort of plan.

Naomi looked awful. Her grey-blonde hair was a ratted mess, her face sheet white and sunken in so you could see her bones, highlighting the dark circles under her beady green eyes. Her thin patchy eyebrows shot up in surprise when she saw Mom walk in with Leslie trailing behind.

"What are you doing here?" Naomi asked in a deep, cracked voice, her hostility on full power despite how weak she looked. Leslie nearly winced at the hate in her voice, but neither Mom nor Amanda—who was standing on the other side of the bed—seemed fazed.

"I came to help your daughter," Mom answered, her tone controlled and expressionless. She was so good at that.

Naomi just scoffed and sipped water out of her Styrofoam cup. "Why? Yours isn't good enough? Gotta steal someone else's too?" She jerked her chin at Leslie, who tried so hard not to react. "Your snobby daughter hasn't had a hard day in her life, has she?"

Leslie shifted on her feet, wishing Mom would just say their goodbyes so she could escape Naomi's heated glare. Instead, Mom stepped even closer to the hospital bed, reached into her purse, then held out a thick roll of what Leslie knew was money. She tilted slightly on her feet and saw the bill wrapped on the outside of the roll was a hundred.

Mom didn't act like she was doing anything special, but Leslie let out a silent gasp. Really, though, she shouldn't have been surprised. Mom was just like that: generous and giving, despite her harsh courtroom persona.

Naomi's face just screwed up with scorn. "I'm not your charity case, Raelyn," she spat. "Save it for when the camera's rollin'."

Mom's face didn't betray her at all. She just nodded, retracted her offering, and pulled Leslie out of the room. It wasn't until the door shut that Leslie saw Amanda had followed them.

Before anyone could say anything, Mom held out the wad of bills to Amanda, who did a double take upon realizing how much it really was.

"Please take it," Mom said, the concern finally showing through her warm brown eyes. When Amanda hesitated, she put the money in her hand and squeezed it. "I don't see you as a charity case, Amanda. I see you as a friend. Please let me help."

Amanda's eyes filled up with tears as she stared into Mom's for a moment before nodding and closing her fist around the money. Then Amanda turned to Leslie.

"I shouldn't have called you," she said, her voice still shaking slightly. "I didn't...I don't know why I freaked out so bad. It's not like this is new or anything. I just...panicked and I shouldn't have."

Leslie shook her head. "No, don't panic about it. It's..." She tried to think of something reassuring and nice to say but came up blank. "It's fine."

"Yeah." Amanda nodded. She gave Mom a nearly grateful nod, then turned to go after the nurse.

Mom took hold of Leslie's arm and led her out of the hospital, which was probably a good thing because it had to have been past two in the morning by now and a wave of exhaustion had overcome Leslie.

The night was warm. Thick. Uncomfortable. Feeling like too much had happened tonight, Leslie was ready to just go home and go to bed and forget all about the dress and dinner and Naomi and the hospital.

They got to their car, but Mom didn't let Leslie go around to the passenger seat. Instead, to Leslie's surprise, Mom pulled Leslie to her chest and squeezed her tight.

"I know we have our problems, Les," she whispered, "but please tell me you know that I love you."

It took Leslie a moment to gather that. Then she nodded as best she could. "Yeah. I know."

She felt Mom kiss the top of her head. "Good." And with that, they got in the car and drove home.

~~~

Amanda didn't go to school the next day. Leslie wasn't surprised. She didn't come the next day either. But on Thursday when Leslie ran into biology, Amanda was sitting in her seat, inspecting her nails and ready to pretend like Tuesday night never happened.

It was relieving to have her back. Navigating life without your best friend was one of the most complicated things in the world.

Unfortunately, though, the complications didn't end with Amanda's return. Thursday night Mom and Dad were leaving for an entire week on business. Seven days of no supervision and Peter running rampant. Leslie would rather get dropped off the edge of Niagara Falls and chewed up by a rhino.
~~~

But it was happening. Both Mom and Dad had business meetings in Los Angeles, so they decided to plan them together and make a trip of it, especially since once the Zambrano case started we would see even less of Mom. So great for them. Misery for Leslie.

Pretty much every time they left town Peter threw a giant party, but last time he got caught and was in major trouble. Somehow that meant that Leslie lost privileges too. Mom left with strict rules for both of them: they were allowed to go to the football game Friday night, but Peter had to take Leslie home right afterward and nobody was allowed to come in or out of the house for the rest of the night. Saturday and Sunday would be the worst since Mom wanted them to pretty much stay home. Besides work and football practice, everyone was expected to come straight home after school and couldn't invite anyone over. Mom would send someone to check on them periodically, but she expected them "to be mature enough to handle the situation largely on their own."

The whole thing irritated Leslie to no end, but when she tried to protest, last Tuesday's dinner was brought up and completely shut Leslie down. Torture won out.

Friday morning was pretty much the same as any other: Peter nearly made them late, they stopped in Make Out City, Megan told Leslie she looked like a gerbil on a cleanse (whatever the heck that was supposed to mean) and Leslie rushed to class. The atmosphere was electric throughout the school; the football game tonight was a big one, playing a huge part in deciding their place in the playoffs. Or, at least, that's what Leslie overheard someone say in the hall.

After school she stowed her backpack in Peter's car, then hung out in the art room and worked on a canvas painting Ms. Mac let her store there. She still hadn't come up with anything for her 'love in death' project, and the deadline was coming up. But even hours of escaping through brushstrokes and pallets didn't give her any ideas.

Elbow-deep in color, it seemed she'd only been painting for fifteen minutes when Amanda popped her head in the door.

"How did I know you'd be in here?" she asked, rolling her eyes. "Game's starting, Picasso. Let's go."

"Coming." Leslie washed her hands in the rainbow-spotted silver sink, grabbed her phone from the counter, and followed Amanda out to the field. They climbed the bleachers to their usual spot—third row in the student section—and Leslie was annoyed to find Amanda was meeting up with people: Findlay, the guy Amanda's had her eye on for a few weeks, and two obnoxious girls Leslie didn't know. The girls just cackled like maniacs over their phones, while Findlay and Amanda were flirting so hard core it was difficult to watch.

So Leslie focused on the field instead. They started out with their new standard: a little memorial type thing for Logan Rasmussen. Three weeks ago during the game, he got hit hard and they rushed him to the hospital because of severe head trauma. He was still in a coma; they weren't sure yet if he was going to pull through. The drill team and cheerleaders did a dance to melancholy song as the football team looked on and people waved their cellphones even though it was still light outside. After a moment of silence and a standing ovation, the game began.

Okay, so it was true—Leslie didn't really know anything about football. She knew to cheer for the guys in gold and hope they got the ball into the right end of the field. That was about it. Usually, she just gauged how good something was by the crowd's reaction and kept her eyes on number ninety-eight, though sometimes she'd glance to number four too. Not that Leslie would know any different, but Clive was a great quarterback.

And, yeah, Peter was pretty good too. It went against every cell in her body to admit it, and nobody would ever catch her saying it out loud. He filled his ninety-eight jersey with the muscles he was so proud of, but he was still surprisingly solid and firm, yet quick and fluid. Leslie had to admit, she was impressed. Her opinion of Peter was dirt high, but you couldn't say the guy didn't work hard when it came to football.

Despite the best efforts of Peter and his team, though, they lost. Bad. The student section was awfully quiet when the last buzzer rang, and the golden jerseys stalked off the field. Slowly, dejected fans started to make their way out of the bleachers and to their cars, crying gold face paint and hanging disappointed heads.

Leslie had lost Amanda about halfway through the first quarter, along with Findlay, and she didn't even want to know what they were doing. She didn't expect to see her for the rest of the night, so she was surprised when she reappeared with her new group, all of them sloshed.

Amanda was wasted, waddling like a penguin caught in ocean waves up to Leslie and spurting something about a party they were going to. She put her arm around Leslie with a huge stupid grin on her face. "You're comin' with us, right Leslie-pie?" she asked, the stench of cheap beer on her breath. "The party is going to be crazy!"

Yeah, hanging out with a bunch of sweaty drunken washouts is just how I want to spend my night.

Leslie wrinkled her nose and sidestepped away from Amanda. "No, I'm going home. I'm supposed to wait for Peter anyway." Who'd have thought being forced to ride with Peter would be useful.

"Are you sure? Maybe Azz-man will be there and give you a big fat—" She smacked her lips against her palm. "Kiss."

"Yeah, completely sure." Leslie hoped Amanda was too drunk to catch all the annoyance her voice emanated. "Bye."

She took out her phone and sat back down on the bleachers, barely offering a wave as the rowdy group made their way off the bleachers.

There's an accident waiting to happen. Now Leslie would have to stay up tonight to see if Amanda would need a ride home. That is, if she herself ever got home and could steal the car from Peter.

She propped her elbows on her knees so she could rest her chin in one hand, then pressed the button to bring her phone to life, scrolling through all her social media feeds. It was pointless, but she had time to burn.

Leslie went through every app she had, learning way too much about others than she cared to know (really, Aunt Karla? Did the world *really* need to see a picture of your ingrown toenail?) then settled on the connect the dots game she'd downloaded during Mr. Bland's history class last year. It wasn't until she won six times in a row that she realized how much time had passed.

Where is he? It wouldn't be surprising if he forgot about her. *I'll just call him.*

She had just tapped the call button next to Peter's name when her screen went black. Phone dead.

"Seriously?" Leslie muttered, pressing power over and over. No luck.

Stupid Peter. I should've just gone with Amanda. It was too far to walk home and she didn't have keys to the car, if it was even still there. Everyone she knew was gone and now her phone was dead.

Really, Peter? Just once could you not try to ruin my life?

With a sigh Leslie stood and slid her useless phone back in her pocket, glancing around. The football field was basically deserted. A group of giggling girls were flirting with some guys across the field, ignoring the couple that was making out behind the bleachers. She heard a commotion to her left and turned to see a small crowd of kids she recognized: black leather, knitted beanies, smelled like a mix of meth, smoke, and near high school dropout—the kind of kids your parents warned you to stay away from.

She accidently met the eyes of one of the guys. He gave her a grin, brushing his stringy shoulder-length blond hair out of his face with a leather-gloved hand. Her blood went icy as she turned and walked as quickly as she could down the bleachers.

Look natural. He has much better things to do than pay attention to you.

"Hey!" someone yelled behind her, making her heart skip a beat. "Wait up!"

Yeah, wait up and die. In a panic she took the last stairs two at a time, but it didn't matter. Punk Blond jumped off the bleachers and landed in front of her, blocking her path. Leslie turned back to the stairs. Three of Punk Blond's friends stood in her way.

Leslie took a shaky breath. *Stay calm. Just stay calm.* She glanced at the small group of people across the field. *Would they even help if they noticed I needed it?*

Punk Blond grinned, taking a step toward her. "Where you going so fast, sweetheart?"

She met his eyes evenly. "Home." She tried to walk past him, but he grabbed her shoulder and pushed her back, and she slapped his hand away.

"Home already?" he asked, his voice ambling, like he was enjoying a long walk. "Don't you want to stay and hang out with us?"

"No thanks. I'm not really into the whole stoner thing anyway."

Leslie pushed past him again. He snatched her wrist and yanked her back, the grin still on his face.

"Why don't you stay and find out?"

She tried to jerk her arm free, but he held on tight, spiking her panic.

"I'm meeting my older brother here," she blurted, her voice nearly squeaking. "He should be here any minute and he'll beat the snot out of you."

Punk Blond just laughed. "Ooh, you hear that boys? He'll beat the snot out of us." The punk boys laughed with him and jumped down the stairs to crowd around him. She tried again to pull her arm free but Punk Blond just tightened his grip. "Now that's somethin' I'd like to see."

Leslie backed away from him, but she only got three steps before she ran into a support beam. "You better leave now," she warned, trying to sound menacing, "before he shows up. He'll—"

"He'll what?" Punk Blond asked, mocking, as he closed the distance between them, still gripping her wrist. "What's big brother gonna to do, huh?"

"Les?" an irritated voice called from a distance. "Les, come on!"

Punk Blond and Co. turned to reveal Peter sauntering up to the field in his letterman jacket, sandy blond hair still crispy with sweat from the game.

"Peter," Leslie breathed in relief. She never thought it'd be possible to be so happy to see him.

He stopped when he saw their small crowd, and his demeanor shifted from offensive to defensive, his eyes narrowing as he looked over Punk Blond's group.

"Oh look," Punk Blond sneered. "It's a football golden boy. Rough game tonight, huh?"

Punch them! Leslie thought, waiting for her savior to save her. *Come on, do something. Smash them like your football people.*

Peter didn't do anything heroic. He shifted his weight before nodding at Leslie, slightly tense but acting as though being held hostage by stoned mouth-breathers wasn't a problem. "Come on, we gotta go."

Fine by me. Leslie took a step forward, but Punk Blond shoved her back against the beam.

"She's gonna stay and hang out with us for a bit, okay big brother? Why don't you find a crowd to cheer you on?"

Peter's jaw locked, but that was the only response he gave. He didn't clench his fists or grab a guy in a headlock or even come up with a good comeback threat.

What are you doing?

Punk Blond laughed. "Not so tough without your posse, huh? Too bad 'cause little sister here was banking on the fact you could hold your own." He gave a sly look to Leslie. "What did you say, sweetheart? He'd beat the snot out of me?"

Peter glanced at Leslie, finally meeting her eyes, and for a terrifying second she thought Peter would actually leave her there. Her mouth fell open with a silent pleading gasp.

"Look," Peter said, still not sounding nearly as concerned as Leslie thought he should be. "I'm taking my sister and we're leaving. End of story." He nodded his head toward the parking lot. "Come on, Les."

Mustering up some courage, Leslie shoved Punk Blond and surged forward, prepared to make a run for Peter, but she only got a few steps before Beanie Guy grabbed her from behind and yanked her back, restraining her against his sweaty body. A squeaky half scream escaped her mouth, and Peter started for her.

"Hey!" he shouted. "Let her—"

Punk Blond socked Peter square in the jaw, making Leslie squeak-scream again. Ticked off, Peter landed two good return hits on Punk Blond, but then the two other stoners joined in, and it went from a scuffle to a fight. Peter held his own for about ten seconds. Then the two guys held him down while Punk Blond hit him over and over.

"Stop it!" Leslie screamed, trying to wrench herself out of Beanie Guy's iron grasp. "Stop it now! Leave him alone!"

She screamed again and again, but no one cared. Amid the chaos, she remembered a moment from the self-defense class Mom had made her take at the rec center years ago. Kicking in a wild panic, she finally nailed Beanie Guy right where it counted. He groaned and dropped to the cement, freeing Leslie, and she dashed to Punk Blond, seizing his arm just as he raised it to punch again.

Bad idea. He just twisted his arm around so he could clamp down on Leslie's, then he used his other hand to slap her across the face. She staggered, hearing Peter's furious protests, and fell to the cement, clutching her stinging cheek.

A new voice was yelling, this one from a lot farther away. Leslie jerked her head up to find Punk Blond and his friends gone, a figure running from the far end of the field toward them. An adult, from the look of it.

"Peter? Peter!" She glanced around everywhere, finding him on the cement a few feet from her where they left him, his face bleeding in at least four different spots and his jaw bruised. The sight of blood was the tipping point: the knot inside her chest seemed to burst open, forceful panic coursing through her body, locking it up, and making her kind of dizzy.

Peter was the opposite. He jumped right up, glancing in the direction Punk Blond must've taken off as he gestured to Leslie. "Get up, let's go," he ordered, his voice low and tight.

But Leslie couldn't get up. Suddenly the cement was too hard and the sky too black and everything too much. She just watched the spot Peter had glanced at and waited for Punk Blond to come back and get them.

"Leslie? Leslie! Get up! Can you hear me? I said go!"

Finally, Peter snatched her wrist and yanked her upright, forcing her forward as he made a break for the parking lot before the shouting adult could catch up. She stumbled, struggling to keep up with the pace. He was hurting her arm. He was going too fast.

He's afraid of them, she realized, almost in awe. *Peter's afraid of someone.*

Somehow they got to the parking lot and found Peter's car. He let go of her wrist and pushed her toward the passenger side.

"Get in."

Leslie froze, rooting herself in the pavement, and didn't move.

"Leslie? Get in the car. Now!"

She heard Peter's words, but she didn't try to compute them. She felt she should run but couldn't find her feet.

Then strong arms were pushing her again. "Leslie, I said get in the car!" Peter jerked open the passenger door and shoved her inside, shutting it again before she could scramble out. Then he was behind the wheel and they were speeding out of the parking lot.

It was quiet. It was too quiet. The outside world blurred past the windows, and Leslie was afraid the car was going to close in on her. Minutes passed. It didn't, but she still waited in terror.

Peter gave a quick sideways glance at her before asking, almost unwillingly, "They didn't hurt you, did they?"

She had to think about that for a second. "No," she answered, her voice small and folded in itself, trying desperately to not be noticed.

He nodded once. Approval, she thought.

More quiet. She folded her arms across her chest and watched the passing streetlights dance over her skin. "You're bleeding," she whispered.

"Yeah, that's what happens when you get hit."

"You're bleeding a lot."

"It's not that much, Les."

More quiet. Leslie turned around to look out the back window. Then she turned back when she felt like she couldn't breathe.

"They're following us."

Peter glanced in the rearview mirror, then relaxed.

"No, they aren't."

"They will."

"No, they won't, Les. Relax."

"No," Leslie insisted, the image painted in her head, vivid color on canvas. "They'll be waiting for us when we get home." Her breaths got faster and lighter at the thought. "They're going to be there waiting for us and we won't be able to get away."

"Do you even know what you're saying right now?" Peter asked, kind of annoyed. "It's crazy."

But it didn't sound crazy to her. She couldn't stop the flow of words and her voice caught. "Yes, they'll be there waiting for us and then you'll bleed everywhere and I'll—"

"That's completely—"

"We can't go home, Peter!" she exclaimed in exasperation, squeezing her hands into tight fists. "We can't!"

"Calm down!" Peter shook his head, still turning down their street despite her objections. "We can go home, okay? Chill."

Leslie nodded because she didn't want him to be mad. Somehow that stressed her out even more.

He glanced at her again. "Jeez, Les, what's wrong with you?"

She clenched her fists tighter. *I don't know.*

They pulled into their garage. The light on the ceiling lit up the entire place, but Leslie knew that there was somehow a corner Punk Blond was hiding.

Peter turned off the car and got out, pausing outside the vehicle when he saw her frozen in the seat. He sighed. "You have to get out now."

Leslie shook her head, two stiff movements. There was no way.

"Come on, Les. Just come inside the freaking house."

"No."

He held up his hands in surrender. "Okay, you know what? Fine. Stay in here for all I care. Just know that if they were hiding out anywhere, it'd probably be in the garage."

It only took a second for that thought to sink in. Then she jerked the door open and dashed to Peter, trailing him inside while watching over her shoulder.

All the lights were off besides the one over the sink, creating odd shadows in the dim kitchen, so when Leslie turned the corner and saw the dark figure on top of the counter, she screamed.

Peter saw it too, but he didn't jump until Leslie screamed behind him. He huffed in irritation, then flipped the light on to show a disgusted and rattled Megan sitting on top of the counter.

She narrowed her eyes and her mouth curled with judgment. "What's wrong with you, freak?"

Leslie usually tried to let those comments slide, but this time she just couldn't. Instead, she made a break for her room.

"Les!" Peter called after her. She didn't stop. "Les, just wait."

She was halfway up the stairs when she heard Megan's awful sugary voice laced with concern. "What happened to you, baby?"

The hallway seemed to stretch on forever. She finally reached her room and slammed the door shut, jumping onto her bed and sitting in a ball. Usually the place seemed too big. Now it was way too small, the walls closing in, the ceiling falling down, and Leslie felt so claustrophobic out of nowhere, so she put a blanket over her head and waited to be crushed.

She could not figure out what was wrong. So, Peter got in a fight. It wasn't the first time—more like the millionth. And it wasn't the first time Leslie had been hit in the face either (when he was twelve Peter went through a karate phase, though he swears now that it never happened). Why was she so freaked out?

She didn't know. But she felt stupid and scared and embarrassed, and she was so overwhelmed that she just started crying right there underneath her blanket. Leslie barely needed both hands to count the times she'd cried since she was eight.

What's wrong with me?

She seriously considered calling Dad to see if he could somehow help, but then she remembered her phone was dead and her charger was in her backpack which was still in the car and there was no way she was ever coming out from under the blanket ever again.

Then her door opened. She stiffened at the sound and held her breath, waiting for the worst. Forty-seven seconds of quiet—she counted—then Peter spoke, making her jump because his voice was almost right next to her.

That was strange. It had to have been years, at least, since Peter was last in her room. She couldn't remember the last time.

"Come out of there, Les." Even without seeing his face, she could feel he was trying super hard to not yell at her for being so annoying.

Leslie sniffed as quietly as she could, then cleared her throat. "Go away."

The blanket started slipping, and she grabbed onto it too late. Her head popped out, bits of her ruined ponytail sticking up in every direction from the static, and she saw him kneeling next to her bed, his face still beaten but now clean of blood.

His expression deflated when he saw hers, as if a whole new rocky mountain for him to climb just presented itself. "You're crying," he stated in obvious discomfort, like he'd been handed a newborn baby and didn't know what to do.

"No I'm not." Leslie shook her head as she wiped away her tears, but they kept coming without permission and she got increasingly frustrated.

Peter rolled his eyes. "I'm not blind, Les. You're crying."

"No, it's…" She racked her brain. "It's a chemical reaction. When a lot of adrenaline leaves your body really fast it has excess build up, and sometimes it uses the tear ducts to create a release. It's called…an emotional overload." She sniffed again. "Maybe if you paid attention in school then you'd know."

Peter wasn't amused. "Uh huh. 'Cause that doesn't sound completely made up at all."

Don't get all smart on me now.

"Just go down and hang out with your pathetic girlfriend," Leslie said, looking down at her hands in her lap, then took a shaky breath. "You don't have to pay me to not tell Mom if you leave me alone."

Peter hesitated. Why wasn't he just leaving? That was an offer Peter had often begged for.

"I, uh, told Megan to leave."

Leslie's gaze flicked back up to him, but he was watching his fingers fiddle with the blanket. That made no sense. "Why?"

He shrugged casually like he was over it, looking at her now. "We aren't supposed to have anyone over anyway. Mom would die." Then he pushed himself to his feet. "I'm ordering pizza 'cause I'm starving. If you want any say on what goes on it, then come downstairs now."

He walked out and she hesitated before calling, "No mushrooms."

She heard him sigh dramatically from down the hall. "Fine."

It took a few minutes for Leslie to work herself up to getting off the bed. She stood in place for a moment, testing the waters, and decided that most of the claustrophobia had gone away. Steps slow and quiet as if to avoid waking anything else, she made her way downstairs. Peter was finishing ordering on the phone—with Mom gone, he would order the good stuff from Pete's and that wasn't something she wanted to miss out on—so she went into the living room and sat on the couch. After a moment, she pulled her legs up too. Somehow, they felt exposed just dangling.

Peter came in once he was done on the phone. "Remote's mine," he called, jumping over the side of the couch and landing on his favorite cushion in the corner. Coincidentally (or not), the remote was right next to him.

Leslie was too tired to object. "Okay."

He glanced at her. "You're not even gonna fight me for it?"

"No."

He turned the TV on before muttering, "Well that's not as much fun."

They ended up watching Attack of the Sharks 2: The Second Wave—one of Peter's favorites—which Leslie thought was the worst movie ever presented to mankind, but she dealt with it.

About a half hour into the movie, the pizza showed up. Leslie didn't move when the doorbell rang, so Peter got the door, voices echoing from the entry, then brought it in the living room with plates and two ginger ales. Peter had gone all out on the pizza: extra cheese, sausage, pineapple, bacon, and pepperoni, but no mushrooms. Leslie forced herself to eat the delicious delicacy as they watched the movie. The third act of the barbaric feature was beginning when she felt she'd finally loosened up.

"That blood is the tackiest thing I've ever seen," she commented, mostly to herself, when a shark ate a guy for the millionth time. "I don't even feel sorry for him."

Somehow that made Peter laugh once. "And she's back."

Leslie tried very hard not to smile.

The rest of the movie was just as absurd as the first half, and she found herself relaxing to the point where she couldn't keep her eyes open. She blinked heavy eyelids, and opened to see all the lights turned off, the movie over, a comedy rerun playing with the volume turned low. Taking a deep breath to reorient herself, she glanced over to find Peter still sprawled in his corner, lazily watching the TV. Probably taking advantage of the fact Mom wasn't here to tell him to turn it off two hours ago.

"Wanna go to bed?" Peter asked quietly when he saw she was awake.

She just groaned at the thought of the stairs, stretched out on the couch, and closed her eyes again.

A banging sound woke her up. Her eyelids fluttered, but then she thought she'd imagined it, wanting to just sleep. Then she heard it again. Louder. Coming from the garage.

Leslie bolted upright to find the TV still on, but Peter was snoring. She had to strain her eyes in the dark, but eventually she read the clock on the wall—it was almost three in the morning. She listened for the sound. It didn't come back. But it wasn't windy outside.

Suddenly wide awake, Leslie slid down the couch until she was sitting next to Peter, then shook his shoulder.

"Peter," she whispered, practically rocking a dead body. "Peter! Wake up!"

He finally threw out his fist—she dodged it—then covered his face with his arms. "Shut up."

Leslie smacked his shoulder. "Wake up."

Peter mumbled something incoherent, then moved his arms and half cracked his eyes open, his groggy voice edgy with resentment. "What do you want, Les?"

She glanced around the dark living room. "I think…I think someone's trying to break in."

He started shaking his head before she was done talking. "Don't be stupid. Go to bed."

"Peter, I really—"

Then there was another sound. Not the same as before, more clanking than smashing, but still most definitely a sound that didn't belong.

Leslie jumped and gasped, hitting Peter's shoulder over and over again and lowering her voice even more. "Peter, did you hear that? There's someone in our garage! There's someone trying to—"

Peter grabbed her smacking hand and tossed it aside. "Will you quit it?"

"Peter, I'm serious." She glanced toward the kitchen, buried in the blackness. "Just go look, okay?"

Despite his best efforts, he was more awake now, and he rubbed his eyes before glaring at her. "You know we have a security system, right?"

She folded her arms resolutely. "I won't leave you alone until I know for sure."

Peter groaned. After another shake from Leslie, he pushed her away and sat up, rubbing the side of his head before standing and heading into the kitchen and toward the garage.

Peter will keep us safe, Leslie reasoned with herself. *It's probably fine.*

But she knew she heard something, and once Peter gave the clear that nothing was wrong, she'd be able to go back to sleep, no problem. Probably. She just needed to relax.

A sliding sounded—fabric against flooring—right behind the couch, and Leslie's heart stopped. Then a looming figure surged up from behind the couch and yelled, making Leslie scream bloody murder.

Then Peter doubled over in laughter.

"You idiot!" Leslie shouted, smacking his head. "You stupid, selfish, freaking *idiot*!"

Her fury didn't even faze him. He could barely get out words in between his hysterical laughter. "You shoulda…you shoulda seen your face!"

"I hate you! I hate you so much!"

Peter finally stopped laughing, wiping little tears from his eyes, and sighed. "That was gold. So worth it." Then he turned to actually head to the garage, and Leslie followed him as far as the kitchen to make sure he did his job this time. She heard the door to the garage open, then swing shut again.

Why did I have to get him as a brother? Why?

Stepping carefully, she wandered through the kitchen and sitting room to the entry, making sure the front door was locked. It was.

Maybe Peter's right. We have a security system. The door's locked. Besides the garage, what else is there?

Leslie heard the slight sigh of the kitchen floor, the almost creak it made when you stepped in the spot by the stairs. Irritation boiling over, she stomped back into the kitchen, ready to chew him out again for trying to scare her.

"Jeez, Peter, what's wrong with…" she trailed off as her eyes adjusted around the new figure standing in the kitchen, then she lost the ability to speak. Because it wasn't Peter standing there.

He was short—probably only a little taller than Leslie—but super thick, probably stronger than Peter. It was the eyes that held her focus though, the black eyes that seemed to somehow glint in the darkness. Eyes of a person she knew could hurt her. Or even kill her.

Leslie opened her mouth to scream, but the man rushed forward and put a finger over her mouth, using his thumb to close her jaw, then brought his other hand to her face. A gun. He was holding a gun. She'd never seen a gun in real life before, and now here one was, aimed at her face in the middle of the night.

Her body froze over, and he tapped his finger against her mouth again. Be quiet or I'll shoot you, he was saying. Leslie nodded a million times. She'd be good. She didn't want to die.

The man lowered his finger from her face, which is when she caught sight of the mark on his bicep, nearly hidden by the sleeves of his black t-shirt. It looked like a web. A spider web.

Zambrano.

Images from Ms. Knudsen's news clips came hurling back at her, all about this man Mom was about to put away forever.

This wasn't just a random break-in. This was revenge.

Her eyes filled with tears, but she was so paralyzed with terror that she couldn't cry them out. They just sat there in her eyes, waiting to die.

A mini almost shriek escaped her when Zambrano began patting her down. He was searching her, she realized. After a few seconds, he pulled her phone out of her back pocket, tossed it on the ground, and stomped on it, sending fragmented pieces all over the floor.

Then the door to the garage opened. Peter's obnoxious voice carried through the kitchen before he got there.

"See, Les, I told you there—"

He skidded to a stop when he rounded the corner into the kitchen and saw the criminal aiming a gun at Leslie.

Zambrano motioned for Peter to come closer. In a daze but with hesitant steps, Peter obeyed, coming around the counter and stopping just a few yards in front of them. Then Zambrano motioned to Leslie's smashed phone on the ground. Peter just stared at them, still in shock. With an impatient huff, Zambrano snatched Leslie's wrist and jerked her to him, wrapping a strong arm to keep her secured against the front of his body, like a shield. She managed to trap her scream but still whimpered when she felt the cold metal gun press against her temple.

"Okay, okay," Peter choked out, his voice frantic as he raised his hands in surrender. "What do you want?" Zambrano pointed to the shattered phone again. Peter's gaze followed this time, and he reached into his pocket, pulled his phone out, and bent down to slide it across the floor. Zambrano lifted his foot and caught the device with his heel.

Peter straightened up and looked to Leslie, disbelief still written all over him. Leslie mouthed the name: *Zambrano.*

Peter's eyebrows furrowed with confusion for a second, then his eyes widened as his face cleared with recognition, right when Zambrano brought his foot down on Peter's phone, effectively cutting off their last reach to help.

Zambrano huffed in what could've been satisfaction, then shoved Leslie forward. His movements were crude and rough to accommodate his bulkiness—no grace but all intimidation—and Leslie barely kept from tripping over her own feet as she walked with him. They stopped right in front of Peter, who didn't seem like he was breathing. Then Zambrano pressed a small, smooth cylinder into Leslie's palm.

She glanced down, finding a syringe full of brilliant blue liquid in her hand. Dread bubbled up in her stomach like bile.

All three of them stood there, still in the darkness, paused in a scene from a horror movie. A nudge from Zambrano finally gave Leslie understanding of what he wanted: he motioned to Peter.

"No," Leslie whispered without sound, shaking her head, as Peter's face drained of what little color it had left in the shadows. "Please no."

Zambrano's black eyes flashed, and he trained his gun on Peter. Leslie's knees started shaking.

"Just do it," Peter muttered through gritted teeth.

Her eyes widened and she shook her head again.

"No! I can't…" Her voice broke. "I can't just—"

"Do it or he'll shoot me." Peter held out his trembling arm. Leslie hesitated, mouth dry, and she heard the deafening click of the gun in the dead silence. "Les, now!"

With a choked shriek, Leslie buried the needle in Peter's arm and jumped away. Zambrano snatched the syringe back, and Peter dropped to the ground. Not dead, though, Leslie realized. His body shook violently, like he was having some kind of seizure.

"Peter!" She pushed herself away from Zambrano and fell to her knees next to Peter, holding his head in her arms. His teeth were chattering harshly, and he looked like a zombie with his eyes half rolled back into his head. "Peter, talk to me! Peter, please!"

A meaty hand wrapped around Leslie's neck and yanked her up, throwing her against the back of the couch.

"No!" Leslie screamed, thrashing every limb with everything she had. "No, no, no!"

Her efforts were useless—Zambrano was an immovable fortress. The blows she put so much power in just bounced off him like annoying flies, and it only took him a moment to lock her down with her arm pinned and exposed.

"You tell your mother," he spat at her with a thick Italian accent, "Zambrano says hello."

Then there was a pinch inside her elbow. Instantly she felt lightheaded and feverish, the vein the needle had protruded getting hot and spicy. Uncomfortable. Burning. The room started spinning slightly, and she felt her body hit the ground when she collapsed, but the harsh bump was a feather duster compared to the all-consuming fire that spread through her body.

She screamed her head off. Or, at least, she thought she did. The world felt faded and distant, as if she were trapped miles under the ocean. An ocean of fire. She felt the presence of her convulsing body, the weight of it, but there was a disconnect, like she was trying to free herself from her incinerated corpse, but something was holding her back, tying her down to her own scorching tomb, and she found herself yearning for the swiftness of Zambrano's gun.

The fire ate at her. Cremated her. Burned her to ash and soot. She blacked out several times, the dark nothingness a merciful relief, but all too soon consciousness would yank her back. Back to the stake. Back to the fire.

Years had passed when the darkness came again, but it was different this time, swooping over her with thick blackness, putting out the flames that licked her but somehow the intensity of heat stayed the same. Like lava. The lava ran over her, blistering in a new way and holding her down. Trapping her. Suffocating her. Then the lava hardened over, burying her in the rock forever.

~~~

It took a long time for Leslie to realize she was awake. That she could open her eyes. One after another, she cracked them open, then hissed and squinted at the burst of light. Slowly, she adjusted, becoming more and more aware of her charred body. Bile rose in her throat as she remembered what had happened. She wasn't sure if she could look.

Hesitating out of fear, she tried to move her fingers. They clenched at her request. Confused, Leslie gradually sat up and inspected herself, expecting the worst. She didn't find a single scratch.

Someone groaned, and she glanced over to find Peter sitting up, then tensing as he looked over himself too. She caught his eye.

"You okay?" he asked warily, as if waiting for the punch line to the strangest joke in history.
~~~

Leslie nodded, clearing her sore throat. "Yeah, but I thought…I thought I'd be…"

"Ash?" Peter supplied.

She shuddered at the thought of the searing pain that was totally gone now. "Yeah." It almost gave her a headache to think about, because she was sure she'd at least have some burn marks after what she just woke from, but her skin was the same as ever.

What in the world?

Going slowly just in case something combusted, Leslie pulled herself to her feet. It felt weird to move her body. Not sore, necessarily, but stiff. New. Like a doll that had just been removed from its packaging and was bending its plastic joints for the first time. She stretched her arms, then scanned around her. Light peeked in from behind the drapes, casting the kitchen in happy and friendly sunlight, a shocking contrast from the dark terror-zone she last remembered. The only evidence of the harrowing encounter was their smashed phones on the floor.

Peter stood too, surveying the room with the same bewilderment on his face that Leslie felt. "What *happened*?"

Leslie glanced down to her arm, finding a tiny hole where she'd been stuck with a syringe, and brushed her fingers over it. "Maybe it was supposed to kill us."

"But I feel fine. If he shot us up with lethal heroin or something and we survived, we'd be feeling it."

Leslie glanced at him. "I don't want to know how you know that."

Peter rolled his eyes. "It's not exactly rocket science, Les. I thought you were smart."

"All I know is five minutes ago, I thought I was dying."

"Yeah." She thought she saw him actually wince. What a tough guy. "Me too."

The doorbell rang, making them both jump. Peter rolled his shoulders and flexed his arms—like he'd just been stretching rather than reacting to the noise—then started for the door.

"Don't answer it," Leslie snapped. "We have no idea who it is."

"I'm hoping it's the cops," Peter bit back, annoyed. "Since our phones are smashed and all. Someone's gotta know that lunatic broke out."

The doorbell rang again, then pounding on the door. Someone really wanted to get in.

Leslie shook her head and folded her arms across her chest. "It's a bad idea. We need to find a phone, call the cops and call Mom."

Peter opened his mouth but was interrupted by the sound of the front door opening.

"Hello? Hey, yo," a male voice called. "Anyone in here?"

Peter stiffened, and they exchanged glances. Who had keys to their house?

"Don't mean to barge in," the guy called again. Leslie heard the door shut and footsteps come down the hallway, the voice getting closer. "Anyone at all?"

Leslie took jerky steps until she was standing behind Peter, unwilling to admit she was hiding behind him. She watched Peter tense up as a man came ambling into the kitchen. Medium height. Thick dark hair. Expensive suit. Probably around thirty but nowhere close to forty.

The guy stopped when he saw them, and a wide, white and nearly perfect smile spread across his face. Fake, Leslie knew. She'd been around rich snobs long enough to know they could afford fake smiles—fake teeth and good intentions included.

"Peter. Leslie," the guy said, looking back and forth between the two of them. "What's going on?"

Neither Peter nor Leslie moved or spoke.

The guy's superior ego faltered, and he gestured to himself. "Bradley Wheeler."

Still nothing.

He pointed to the Bluetooth in his ear. "I work with your mom. Raelyn. You guys used to come visit the office when you were kids. You'd steal my blow pops."

Peter relaxed, so Leslie did too. That made sense, snobby attitude and suit included.

"You guys really don't remember me?" Bradley asked, his superficial tone covering up hurt. "Huh. Okay, then. Not much for confidence, but what can ya do?" He cleared his throat, as if getting back to business. "You guys wanna tell me what's going on?"

"What do you mean?" Peter asked, way too fast. That guy was always on the defense. Never wanted to get in trouble.

Bradley laughed once. "Your mom sent me to check on you, you know, since you're on your own and all." He gave another smile. "You can tell me what's really going on. I'll give an edited version to your mom." Then he winked at them, like he was in high school and they were all best buds or something dumb like that.

"What do you mean 'going on'?" Leslie asked, not understanding.

Bradley laughed again and gave her a smile. He smiled too much. Leslie hated people that smiled too much. "Nice one, kiddo, but I think we all know

Mondays are for school and it's—" He paused to check his watch. "One in the afternoon and I found you here after the school called Raelyn. She said you guys wouldn't answer her calls." He rubbed his hands together. "So, what, are you guys just sluffing? Rebel against the parents and all that jazz?"

Leslie blinked in shock. "It's *Monday*?"

Bradley nodded, one fast motion. "Monday afternoon, to be exact."

"But that…that doesn't make any sense." It had just been Friday night. Sure, the burning drug of death seemed to last years, but not days.

What happened to us?

Bradley laughed. Again. "Funny, Leslie, because last time I checked, Monday always came after Sunday despite all of our tireless efforts." Then his smile faded. "You guys okay? You're acting kinda strange."

Peter shook his head. "You know Zambrano?"

"Zambrano? As in Julian Zambrano?" Bradley laughed but without amusement. "Yeah, he's only making our office go 'round right now."

"He broke out," Peter said. "He came here Friday night, probably trying to get us to get at my mom."

All of the fake friendliness drained out of Bradley, and he was suddenly more serious than Leslie would've thought he was capable of. "Are you guys okay?"

Peter and Leslie nodded at the same time. "I think so," Leslie said. "But I don't get it: he just shot us up with something and left. Why didn't he kill us? Or at least take us for ransom. Our parents would've paid anything for us."

Bradley raised an eyebrow. "He injected you with something?"

Peter nodded, rubbing the back of his neck. "Some wicked blue Kool-Aid."

"He injected both of you."

They nodded again.

"And you both feel…?"

Peter shrugged. "I feel fine now."

Leslie nodded in agreement. "Me too."

Maybe even better than fine. She had to admit she'd never felt more alert. Her fingers tingled with a new kind of life she couldn't place. *Maybe I'm making it up.*

Their answers only made Bradley impatient. He stepped forward to put an arm around both of them and pulled them toward the front door. "We need to get out of here immediately, in case Zambrano changes his mind and comes back for you. I'll let the cops know he's out, and your mother that you're both safe and with me."

Leslie protested for shoes, and eventually Bradley complied, following as they both went to the mud room off the garage to grab their sneakers.

"Lace 'em up in the car," Bradley said, urging them onward. "It's a miracle you guys have lasted as long as you have unprotected."

They were rushed out into the sun, the blinding rays springing off the bright cement, and into Bradley's silver convertible. Peter assumed control in the passenger seat, and Leslie got settled in the back as Bradley raised the roof on the car and started driving.

Leslie tried not to get her dirty shoes on the expensive tan leather seats, which made tying the laces even harder, but she managed. Making a rabbit, just like Dad had taught her.

"Are our parents coming home?" Leslie asked Bradley.

Bradley nodded. "They're on a plane right now."

"Shouldn't we get to a doctor or something?" Peter asked, flexing his arm. "I feel fine, but we still got something pretty bad inside us."

"We're headed there now," Bradley answered. "A buddy of mine is a specialist."

The word confused Leslie. "A specialist of what?"

Bradley glanced at her in the rearview mirror, holding her gaze. "Zambrano is a major drug dealer. Into lots of nasty stuff. A lot of it new too, stuff Zambrano doesn't fully understand, which is why we need to find someone who does." He shook his head. "Just because you feel fine now doesn't mean something isn't going to show up later." He paused. "Nobody's itchy or hallucinating yet, are they?"

Leslie thought for a moment. "No."

"Me either," Peter said.

Bradley nodded. "Good."

They drove for a long time—almost two and half hours—nearly to Phoenix. Leslie watched the clock, willing it to go faster. Peter had assumed control of the radio, seeming at ease despite the uncomfortable situation, and Bradley had given up on getting to know her an hour ago. Her fingers twitched, aching for her sketchbook. She didn't feel right; she just wanted out, to be home, with Mom and Dad, safe. If the impatience for the ride to be over didn't kill her, then she was going to be overpowered by the cherry vanilla car freshener that was way too potent for any normal person.

"Why are we going so far?" she finally asked when they were twenty minutes out of the big city.

"I apologize for the drive," Bradley said. "I promised Raelyn I'd get you the best care I know. My buddy's in Phoenix for the day on business."

"Is he going to know what to do for us?"

"I hope so, kiddo. He's the best in the business. It's a big deal he'll take the time to see you."

Leslie rolled her eyes. *What a saint.*

"Is he busy when he comes to Phoenix?"

Bradley's nod came a little late. "It's his busiest stop."

"Then why—"

"Will you just shut up and be grateful?" Peter cut in, exasperated. "Or we'll leave you on the side of the road."

"Fine," Leslie muttered, fixing her eyes out the window again.

When Bradley finally stopped, it was in the parking lot of some kind of warehouse on the outskirts of Phoenix, several workers transporting crates onto big supply trucks. He turned to look at both of them and tapped his Bluetooth apologetically.

"Important work call. Sensitive information." He grinned. "But you guys are probably familiar with that drill now, aren't you? Hang on for a sec." He turned the engine off but left the car on, so they'd still have air conditioning, then stepped out and shut the door behind him. Leslie could hear his muffled voice from yards away as he answered his call.

"Do you think something's wrong with us?" Leslie asked Peter. She couldn't help herself. Everything was just too weird today.

Peter gave a long dramatic sigh, like he couldn't believe she was still there. "It'll be fine, Les. Chill, will you?"

She turned her attention back to Bradley Wheeler, still standing and talking outside the car. His back was to them, so she couldn't see his face or read his lips, and she wondered what was so important to him.

Curiosity got the best of her. She tapped the button on her car door, barely cracking open her window. Peter sighed again but didn't say anything.

"Nothing at White's place yet, huh?" Bradley was saying, his voice animated. Charismatic. The rich guy wanted something badly, and it was something he couldn't buy. "How long are they staying? I got two fresh ones, just days old. I'm not a hundred, but I'm ninety-nine, and that's the next best thing, isn't it?" He paused. "It's worth a look, though, right?"

Then Bradley started turning. Leslie jumped and quickly rolled up her window, then inspected her nails, feeling Bradley's eyes on her.

"He said he works for Mom," Peter said before she could speak. "He's a slime ball, but he's in charge."

But Leslie didn't feel right. "Yeah, and he also said he was taking us to his doctor buddy, not some loading warehouse."

"You need to stop whatever you're doing. This new weird paranoia thing you've got going on is getting old."

Leslie gritted her teeth and slammed back against the seat, folding her arms across her chest and pretending like the remark didn't sting.

Bradley walked back to the car and opened his door, leaning in to grab the keys out of the ignition.

"All right, come on out. My buddy's a lifesaver and agreed to meet us here." He gave Leslie a knowing glance. "Don't worry; we aren't trespassing. The law firm owns this warehouse. You're safe here. Heck, just mention you know Raelyn and these guys will be lining up to be your best friend." Tipping his head back, he laughed like that was the funniest joke in the world. His head caught the top of the car on his way out, and Leslie had to hold back a laugh of her own as he reoriented himself. She got out of the backseat and bit the inside of her cheeks.

The hot sun sent a stinging sensation up her arms after hours of air conditioning. Leslie glanced around the parking lot, noting the beefy men in tank tops, sweat soaking their faces, loading crate after crate into supply trucks. Most didn't spare her a second glance, but a few of them watched her with interest. There was no hint of admiration or excitement or insincere friendship, like she was used to. The only emotions she could pick out were either disdain or pity.

Leslie's shoulders tensed with irritation. Didn't they realize who she was?

Peter didn't like it either. His mouth pulled into a frown as his eyes skirted the area while Bradley ushered him forward. They went through the parking lot and into a vast garage, which was where a man in a crisp pinstriped suit—a stark contrast from the workers—was waiting.

"Basil Hartman in the flesh!" Bradley exclaimed, clapping his hands together. "Wonderful to see you, sir."

"Wheeler," Basil greeted, his mousy face narrowed with cold calculation, as if his eyes could frost over Bradley's enthusiasm. "I hope you're not kidding around about this."

Leslie bounced on her heels, waiting to be introduced so she could just get this over with and go home, but Bradley acted like they weren't even there.

"Not kidding, Hartman. I've got something here, at least."

"I believed you, I acted for you, and we're here. Don't let me down, Wheeler. For both our sakes."

"I get it."

Finally, Basil's eyes turned on Leslie and Peter, making them both stiffen. He watched them for a moment, the same disgusted contempt in his expression the workers had, before he regarded them curtly. "Well, then. Follow me."

Leslie did not like the idea of going anywhere with Basil Hartman—much less be helped by him—but when Peter and Bradley started walking, she decided to follow rather than have Peter yell at her.

This'll be over soon. This'll be over and then you can go back home.

Once inside, Leslie found the warehouse to be largely empty: hundreds of towering shelves with only a handful of metal crates dotting along. High above them, skinny frosted windows lined the top of the walls by the ceiling, offering sunlight but no look into the outside world, and the air was too hot and stuffy. The workers must've used a different side to actually pack and move, because they only passed two guys talking on their way. Basil's steps were long and purposeful, and Leslie struggled to keep up, especially since Bradley walked right behind her. If she slowed any, he'd bump right into her.

Jeez, give me some space.

Basil led them past all the shelves and into a back room that could've been a conference room except there was no table. A few rusty foldup chairs were set up haphazardly throughout the space. Bradley dragged one next to the other, both of them facing the door, then pushed Leslie and Peter into them.

"Wait here," Bradley ordered, his voice harsher than normal. He held up a finger. "Do not leave this room, capisce?"

They nodded, and the men left, shutting the door behind them.

"This is weird," Leslie said under breath after a moment of unsettling silence.

Finally, Peter agreed. "Yeah. This is weird."

It was hard to wait, even for a second. Leslie started tapping her foot, quick slaps against the hard floor. Peter hit her leg to get her to stop. She huffed in frustration but stopped.

How long do we have to stay here? she wondered. *Shouldn't Mom and Dad have landed by now?*

She was about to knock on the door and ask what the heck was going on when she heard footsteps approaching on the other side.

"So?" she heard Bradley ask, his tone colored with pathetic hope.

"One chance," Basil answered. There was still no expression to his voice. "That's all you're going to get."

Even from here, Leslie could sense Bradley struggle to maintain his excited relief. "Of course. That's all it should take, right?"

Do they know we can totally hear them?

Basil took a breath. "Yes, I suppose." There was a fraction of a pause. "They don't know a thing, do they?"

"From what I got so far, no," Bradley responded. "Formula got mixed up with another clueless dealer. Parents are out for the week—high profile, but by the time they get back, the kids will be just another missing case."

Leslie froze when she realized he was talking about them.

"Security tapes at their house show the guy breaking in," Bradley went on. "Authorities'll be pointed that way for the foreseeable future. Nobody is going to find these kids." Someone clapped their hands together. "It's too perfect."

Leslie gave a silent cry and looked to Peter, who slipped his cover for a second and had his mouth hanging open in fearful disbelief.

"Peter," Leslie whispered, dangerously close to freaking out. "Peter, what do we do?"

He didn't answer. He just sat there, still, eyes wide. "Peter?"

"Do you know how the dealer got his hands on the formula?" Basil asked, accusing, like it was all Bradley's fault.

A beat of silence. "No," Bradley admitted. "Not yet, but we're tracing the trail. Shouldn't be too long until we find out."

Voices started up again, including Bradley's, but it was farther down the hallway and harder to make out. Leslie strained her ears, trying to pick up on any helpful information. She'd read Mom's cases and research. She knew how many kidnapped kids were lost in mounds of paperwork and buried in shattered hearts, never found.

Leslie could not be one of those kids.

Heavy, powerful footsteps sounded, getting closer as the voices got louder and more defined. Leslie clutched the edges of her chair as her heart hammered in her chest and the door swung open.

Instead of mousy Basil Hartman or fake Bradley Wheeler, as expected, four unfamiliar men came through, carrying triple the power—or maybe even more—than Mom did when nailing someone down in the courtroom. Two of the men hung in the back, as if acting as guards. The other two were dressed in similar black and violet suits, clearly the two in charge, though besides their clothing and dark hair color they could not have been more different from each other.

The taller one was all angles and boxy muscles, a hard face framed by shoulder-length wavy hair. His inky eyes were something inherently heinous yet dynamic, something Leslie would never be able to paint or recreate even with the best supplies, even if she saw those eyes in every nightmare for the rest of her life. They were open and inviting, addicting, luring, but only into a tomb: cold, hateful, and deadly.

Those eyes held Leslie hostage. She felt she was suffocating under his stare, and somehow she knew she'd never breathe again.

By the arrogant jerk of his chin, he announced himself as the leader of the room. However, it was his counterpart that did all the talking. This man was shorter and rounder, reduced to leaning on a silver-adorned black cane because of his obvious limp, though he didn't seem to rely completely on it. His eyes were wider. Animated. Manic.

"What do we have here?" Cane Man asked, delighted, as he looked over Leslie and Peter, who were paralyzed. "Two with one stone, you found, uh—" He turned toward the open door. "Wheeler, was it?"

At that, Hartman and Bradley came in. "Yes, sir," Bradley answered, standing up straighter than he had all day. "Siblings, sir. Accidental crime infection."

Cane Boy turned back, and Leslie couldn't help a wince upon meeting his eyes. "You don't say. Those are becoming much too frequent, sadly."

The Leader's unfeeling expression didn't change. He just watched Leslie and Peter for a minute with awful, paralyzing eyes, then gave a curt nod.

"Well, I must say," Cane Boy went on. "This is impressive. Siblings always make for an interesting dynamic, in what little we've found." He turned to face Wheeler. "Hartman will input their information, and you'll be promoted to handler status." He reached his free hand out to shake Bradley's. "Congratulations, Wheeler."

Bradley tried not to smile, but his countenance beamed as he shook the small hand. "Thank you, Jefferson, sir. I won't disappoint."

Then the entourage left as suddenly as they came, leaving Hartman and Wheeler. Once Leslie was free from the Leader's terrible glare, she realized she hadn't moved or breathed or thought, really.

"Who are you?" Peter demanded once the two scary guys and their detail were gone. His hands clenched into fists, finally ready to fight. "You've been lying to us, and it stops now."

Wheeler just laughed, the sound scornful now rather than the haughty chuckle she'd endured all afternoon—had it only been one afternoon? "That's cute, kid, but the charade is over." Leslie heart stopped when he reached into his expensive jacket and pulled out a gun, her mouth drying up when he waved it at them. "Let's go."

Leslie's eyes never left the gun, and somehow that made it really hard to breathe. Everything went by in a blurry whirlwind—suddenly she was walking, Bradley roughly dragging her along, still not explaining anything despite Peter's angry questions. She vaguely remembered wanting to scream in protest when they were separated, but she didn't know if she actually vocalized anything. She found herself without Peter, alone in a room with Bradley, who pushed her up onto a machine—a treadmill type thing, she finally realized—and zip tied her wrists to the railings. Then he brought the machine to life, a screen with a bunch of diagrams lighting up, and he started sticking ten different pieces of plastic to her skin, all attached to the machine by thin black cords: four on her head, two on her neck, four on her chest. A dot on the screen flashed in time with her pounding heart.

"What's going on?" she asked, finally finding her voice.

"Congrats, kiddo," Bradley responded with a smile. Leslie knew that smile had been fake. "You're infected now. You're different. And we need to find out just how far you can go—I bet you'll even surprise yourself." He finished hooking her up, then clapped his hands together. "Start running."

She actually managed to glare at him. "Or what?"

Bradley smirked and pressed a button on the machine. Ten different spots on her skin scalded, jolting her with nasty bursts of electricity that made her half shriek and half choke.

Leslie started running.

~~~
~~~

The floor was warm. She wished it were cold. She needed something cold.

The warm floor was smooth underneath her exhausted body as she was dragged down the hallway. She watched the shoes of a man she didn't know pull her by her arm, barely able to hold a coherent thought. Except hurt. Everything hurt.

Shoes stopped. Something creaked. More dragging, then she got dropped to the warm floor. More creaking as the footsteps left. Leslie couldn't lift up her head to check, but she thought she was alone now.

She didn't move. She just waited, face down, sprawled out on the warm cement floor, muscles she didn't even know she had aching in ways she didn't know a human body could ache. Throbbing. They throbbed. Pulsed. She felt she might explode if she had the energy for that kind of combustion.

Time passed. Muscles throbbed. She finally became aware of her short, quick gasping, the wispy sound alone in the empty air. And her heart pounding. It was starting to slow. It was exhausted too.

Eventually there was a bang, then footsteps. She whimpered, but she couldn't hear her own sound over the purposeful steps. Creaking. Farther from her, but close. Short quick gasping. Like hers. Then more footsteps, slowly fading away.

Using a remarkable amount of the tiny bit of life she had left, Leslie turned her head, resting her cheek against the warm cement floor, and searched until her eyes found Peter in the cell next to her. His head hung forward as he leaned on hands and knees and threw up. Leslie waited, knowing it would pass. She'd thrown up three times—or maybe four—but now there was nothing left.

She watched a chip on the cement a few inches from her face until the gross sounds stopped and Peter collapsed onto the ground. Her throat was cracked and dry and itchy, but she still managed to choke out a raspy whisper.

"Are you okay?"

Peter grunted, rolling over on his side to look at her. "Do I *look* okay?"

How does he have the strength to still be a jerk?

She ignored his tone. "Me neither. I've never…" She shuddered, and the movement made her whimper. "I've never run like that before."

"I haven't either. Not in practice. Nothing. I don't…I don't think normal people can run like that."

She took a shaky breath, letting it fill up her lungs and expand her body, willing it to feel better. "What do we do?"

"I…" Peter sighed and closed his eyes. "I don't know, Les."

Leslie blinked in surprise. "What do you mean you don't know?"

"I mean—"

"We have to get out of here," Leslie insisted, new panic rising. "We have to—Peter, what happens when they get tired of running us? What comes after that? It's like…"

"Experimentation," Peter supplied bitterly. "I heard Bradley talking. Whatever Zambrano put in us, it changed us. They call it infection. It makes us stronger. Faster. Not a ton, but enough to be different."

"Infection." Leslie tried the word out, hating the way it formed on her lips, but it confirmed her suspicions. She really didn't want to believe it, but she felt something was wrong with her. Was she about to sprout wings or a second head or suddenly be able to shoot lasers out of her eyes? "Why are we here? Are we dangerous?"

Peter shook his head. "Not us. We're just more durable. They're looking for one—a key. A monster. Whoever finds it gets a huge payday. They want to weaponize it." He spat on the ground as though spitting on the key itself. "The rest of us are just mistakes."

"So Bradley hopes it's one of us?"

"I told him we weren't. He didn't believe me. Shocking, I know."

"Eventually they'll figure it out though, right? We aren't. And then they'll leave us alone." As much as she needed to believe that, her voice fell flat.

Peter sighed. "I don't know. These are bad guys, Les." He sounded like he was going to say something else but stopped himself.

Mom deals with bad guys all the time, Leslie reasoned with herself, trying to ignore the fact that Mom probably didn't know what was going on since Bradley was a big fat liar. *Mom deals with real bad guys all the time and we've been fine so far.*

This all felt like a dream. A nightmare. Unreal. It couldn't be real. How bizarre did being an 'infected' sound anyway?

It's not real. It's not.

The bang sounded again—a door opening—and Bradley's pathetic voice echoed down the hallway, brimming with pride.

"Come on, Hartman, this is big!" he was saying, getting closer and closer. Leslie took a page out of

Peter's book and pretended to be unconscious. "I've been chasing the formula through cartels for four years now. Four *years*. I deserve to move up. I've earned it." His tone went darker as he muttered, "Unlike others."

Hartman hummed in agreement. "We can't all be Sark."

"No, we can't."

The footsteps and voices stopped in front of Leslie's cell. Or so she thought. She didn't even dare peek through her eyelashes to see, the fear of pain paralyzing her. The burn in her body was subsiding, her energy bouncing back like the snap of a rubber band in slow motion, ready to be annihilated again by whatever heinous experiments Bradley would come up with. That was insane. She'd been run to death. She shouldn't have been able to move ever again.

What did they do to me?

"They're both out?" Bradley questioned, nearly annoyed.

Hartman's voice lacked any form of patience— Bradley was getting on his nerves. Finally, something Leslie could agree with. "If your report was correct, they're days old. It will take time for them to get used to their bodies as they are now. That should be common knowledge to someone so seasoned."

Leslie could feel the remark shut down Bradley's animated vibe. "Yes, sir. Of course, sir."

Bradley is new at this—whatever 'this' is. She imagined him like Shelbee Rubes—the president of teacher's pets—so smart, yet so senseless, and so eager to please. *Hartman knows Bradley's in over his head.*

"Best of luck to you," Hartman said with a flat voice, clearly hoping Bradley crashed and burned and blew away in the wind. "We'll be in touch."

"Yes, sir," Bradley mumbled. One set of footsteps trailed away. A loud creaking sounded. She felt him get closer to her, and he even nudged her shoulder with his shoe.

Don't move. Stay calm. Stay calm. He thinks you're asleep. It's okay.

"Wheeler!" a voice called in the far distance.

"Yeah!" Bradley yelled back, quick footsteps retreating, creaking and slamming following. Leslie peeked her eyes open to see he had slammed the gate too hard—instead of closing, it had hit against the frame and bounced back, leaving it cracked open.

"When he comes back," Peter whispered to her, "you gotta grab his gun."

"What?" Leslie gasped. "No way. I'm not touching that thing."

"How else are we going to get out of here?"

"Oh, so, what, you're going to shoot the place up?"

"Of course not," Peter scoffed. "But we need some sort of intimidation."

She rolled her eyes. "That's not what we need. We need to sneak out." Painfully, she crawled to the wall of her cell and grabbed onto the bars, using them to pull herself up. Then, stepping carefully, she opened the cell door as slowly as possible to avoid creaking, just enough that she could slip out.

"Hartman thinks Bradley's a moron," Leslie reasoned. "A newbie. This will be our only chance to sneak out before he learns."

Sliding a bobby pin out of her ponytail, Leslie bent it straight and unlocked Peter's cell—she had years of practice breaking into Peter's cabinet, when he would hoard the good food or hide her stuff he stole. Then they were off, tiptoeing down the hallway opposite of where Bradley had gone. They followed it until a green 'Exit' sign pointed left, which led them through double doors and in the backside of the parking lot.

Leslie glanced around the empty lot wildly, wondering what to do, but Peter found an emergency phone attached to the wall by the corner of the warehouse. He dialed 911 immediately. Leslie stood next to him and bounced on her toes, glancing over her shoulder every few seconds, waiting for a warehouse working to come around the corner and expose them.

"Yeah, my name's Peter Wyman," Peter said into the phone, keeping his voice quiet. "My mom is Raelyn Wyman, the prosecutor. My sister and I were kidnapped—we need a cop to pick us up now, before we get caught again." He quickly glanced at the road signs, gave the address for what would be the corner two blocks down, then hung up. "Let's go." She followed him without question, eager to leave the warehouse of horrors behind.

They had to wait at the designated corner for five minutes—easily the longest minutes of Leslie's life— before a cop car pulled up. The guy rolled down his passenger window, leaning over the seat. "You kids the Wymans?"

Leslie nodded in relief, and the cop motioned for them to get in the backseat. Peter shoved her inside before jumping in himself, then they told the cop to drive far away. Somewhere safe.

"We can't go home yet," Peter explained. "They know where we live."

The cop nodded, thankfully taking them seriously.

"I understand. I'll take you downtown to the station and we can watch you there while we get your stories and figure this out."

It was a ten minute drive through the streets of downtown Phoenix to get to the police station. Leslie kept her head down, watching her one knuckle that was about to crack, afraid to look out the window and expose herself. The cop wasn't very talkative—probably giving them space—but turned up the radio so they could listen to his country music. She had to hold back a groan.

When they parked in the lot of the police station, the cop told them to wait in the car for a moment while he got everything set up, then got out and disappeared a few feet to the left, right around the corner of the building. That didn't seem right.

Leslie leaned over, trying to get a glimpse of what he was doing. She could see the cop standing there, his back to her, and he seemed to be talking to someone. She leaned farther. Then her heart stopped. Her hands went numb and prickly.

"Peter!" she gasped, but her fear had taken her voice. She hit Peter's shoulder over and over again, unable to rip her eyes away from the scene, as she cleared her throat and tried again. "Peter, it's Bradley!"

"What?" Peter leaned over, and she heard a harsh breath go through his teeth when he saw the police officer talking to Bradley, exchanging something.

Bradley paid him off.

Peter opened his car door as quietly as possible, then yanked on Leslie's arm, stepping out of the car and making a break for anywhere. The knot was tight in Leslie's chest as she ran after Peter, down the blocks, past the buildings, past the people. Normal, average people. Leslie had just been one of those. And now a random police officer was turning her in to deranged psychos for experimentation.

The thought dawned on her as Peter grabbed her arm again and yanked her into an alley between a restaurant and dentist office.

We can't trust anyone. Because any single one of those 'normal, average people' could be working with Bradley.

Leslie leaned against the wall and slid to the ground, curling into a ball. Her head spun around and around, and she felt like she was going to throw up again.

We can't trust anyone.

"Let's keep going," she heard Peter say. "Come on."

But even if she wanted to, she couldn't move. She couldn't get up. She felt cemented where she was, spinning around and around, unable to get a good grasp on anything.

Peter gave an exasperated sigh. "No, Les, not this crap again." She felt a tugging on her shoulder. "Come on!" Harder tugging and louder words. Leslie curled tighter. "We don't have time for this! Now!"

She put her hands on either side of her head and whispered, "Stop yelling at me."

Another loud sigh, then a smacking sound. He probably hit something. Leslie just stared at a small rock next to her shoe, shoulders heaving with labored breaths, as she waited for something to kill her.

It could be anything. It could be anyone. I can't trust anyone.

A few moments passed before Peter kneeled down in front of her, tilting his head until he was eye level with her.

"What's wrong, Les?" he asked, his voice tight with forced patience.

She couldn't find the right words to explain. How could she? So after several seconds of watching Peter get increasingly annoyed, she finally whispered, "I'm scared."

That brought the annoyance to a halt. His eyes widened with…fear. Peter was actually afraid. "I know, I…" His strong voice faltered. "I am too. A lot." He cleared his throat. "But you can trust me, okay? When I say run, you gotta run. Fast." He tapped her shoulder. "You can probably keep up with me now, if you try. We've got to use this freak show to our advantage when we can."

There was only one part of that Leslie cared about.

"I can trust you?"

Peter nodded. "Yeah, you can. You know that, right? We can go now?"

"I don't know." Out of all the people she knew, Peter was at the bottom of the 'trust' list. "I don't think…"

"Well, you can," Peter snapped, the ounce of patience he found now used up. "Let's go."

"Will you let me get caught?" Leslie asked uncertainly.

"No, Les." He shook his head in frustration. "Why would you even think that? You're making stuff up again."

"But you've said that before," she insisted. She couldn't just let this go. "You've said I'm annoying and useless and it would be better if I never went home." The alley was getting smaller and smaller, she could've sworn. "You said that. All the time. You could leave me behind."

Peter's face seemed to fall as his eyebrows shot up. She'd surprised him. She couldn't read the expression on his face though, as he tried to stammer through a response.

"Well, that's...I mean, that's...that was just kidding around, Les. You weren't supposed to...actually take that seriously."

"Oh."

She didn't say anything else. She couldn't think of anything else to say, so she just sat there. Eventually Peter rolled back from his knees onto his feet, then turned around and sat next to her, leaning against the wall. Leslie heard the sound of cars whizzing past yards outside of the alley. She wished she could get in one of them. She wished Mom and Dad were here.

"What does it feel like," Peter asked out of nowhere, his voice quiet, "when you freak out like that? What's happening?"

Leslie had to take six breaths, calculating the weight of each word. "I don't know. I just...I feel like I can't breathe. And everything spins and closes in, like...something will crush me. And everything seems so much scarier and so much more...real." She took a deep breath, starting to feel better. "And I know it doesn't make sense. I know it's irrational. But it happens. And I don't make it up, I swear." She glanced sideways at him, but it was too fast to actually see his expression. "Do you believe me?"

"Yeah, I guess." He hesitated. "You're not really the type to make this up."

Leslie nodded. That was the truest thing she'd ever heard him say.

Shaking her head a few times, she stretched out her arms, popping her neck, then relaxed. "It's over now. Where…" She sighed, remembering their situation. "What should we do?"

Peter hit his fist against his palm over and over again as he thought. "Call Mom. She's gonna…" He laughed once, derisively. "She's gonna freak."

"Is she even going to believe us?" She tapped her fingers together. "But we can't go home. We can call to let her know we're okay, but we can't meet up with them or go…" She sighed. "Bradley could track us anywhere. He's probably expecting us to call Mom."

"Yeah, but…we're gonna need some help. With everything. I can—"

"No," Leslie interrupted, turning to look at him head on. "We aren't calling one of your brainless friends. You can't even call them friends."

Peter's eyes narrowed. "What other option do we have? The two losers you hang out with?"

Leslie scoffed. "Any one of your 'friends' would give us up for fifty bucks. Duane would do it for twenty." Peter opened his mouth to argue, but then stopped himself. Leslie gave a tight smile. "You know it's true. We can trust Amanda and Chet—I know we can."

He shook his head. "I won't be caught dead with them—"

"Get off your high horse, moron. This is bigger than your ego." She paused, getting serious. "Besides, if you want me to trust you then you have to trust me too."

Peter let out a long dramatic sigh, rubbing his forehead. "Fine. But if this backfires, it's on you."

"Fine." Leslie dragged herself to her feet, Peter following suit. "What phone are we going to use? Even if we're lucky enough to find another payphone, we won't have any money."

Peter squared his shoulders and puffed out his chest. "I can take care of that." He peeked around the corner of the alley for a minute before walking out onto the sidewalk, steps confident but still ambling, and Leslie did her own survey down the street before scampering after him.

"Look natural," Peter muttered under his breath to her. "You're trying way too hard."

She tried to force her legs to bend normally, her shoulders to sit straight, her head forward instead of checking behind her shoulder. Her eyes still darted everywhere though. At the blonde in exercise clothes pushing a stroller. At the parents with three kids all licking ice cream cones. At the old man walking with his Great Dane.

Where are you, Bradley?

They ended up at a café where dozens of people were enjoying drinks and sandwiches and pastries in the courtyard. Peter strolled right up to a table of three girls in big sun hats and tiny shorts, pulling up a chair and cutting their conversation short.

"Hey ladies," he said, his voice dripping with what he thought was charm. "Sorry to interrupt, but I couldn't help noticing a table full of beauties like yourselves."

Leslie had to keep from rolling her eyes. *Oh brother.*

She stood there trying to look natural (and not annoyed) as Peter flirted it up with the girls, who just smiled and giggled and flirted right back. It was disgusting. Why any right-minded female would even tolerate Peter, let alone like him, was a complete mystery.

But the fake charm worked. Not only did Peter get all of the girls to offer their phones for a call, he even scored glasses of water from the waiter. Leslie did her absolute best to drink it slowly, even taking breaks in between sips, instead of chugging it down with ferocity like she wanted to. Then Peter took her aside so they could make their call.

Leslie reached for the phone, but Peter kept it out of her reach. She huffed in frustration and folded her arms as he dialed a number and brought the phone to his ear. He waited. Leslie tapped her foot against the ground. His expression faltered for just a moment before he started talking.

"Hey Mom, it's Peter. You guys are probably in a meeting or something, I guess." He sighed. "That's probably a good thing. Okay, well something happened. Something kind of big. And I…I'll have to tell you about it later, but the point is Les and I have to disappear for a few weeks while we figure this out. We'll come back soon, you just can't go to the police, okay? I'm serious, Mom, you have to just wait this one out. We'll be safe and be home in a couple weeks. Don't worry." Peter's eyes flicked to Leslie for just a moment. "I'll take care of, Les. We'll see you soon." Then he pressed the end button. Leslie went to take the phone, but suddenly his eyes lit up and he started dialing another number.

"What are you—" Leslie started.

"Hayden!" Peter burst out, leaking desperation everywhere. Leslie's heart swelled at the thought of her uncle on the line. "I'm so glad you answered. We need…has anyone contacted you? Any kind of stranger asking about us?" There was a moment as he listened. "Good. Okay, yeah that's good. It's just…we're in trouble. And we need to skip town for a while."

Uncle Hayden must've said something Peter didn't like, because Peter's face went pale and his eyebrows ruffled in defensive anger. "No! No, it's not like that again, I swear. I know…No, I know. Yeah. I know. It's just that we—" His eyes flicked to Leslie for a second. "Yeah, she's with me. It's not what you…I know. I know! I've got her. You don't have to—" He deflated, pursing his lips into a thin line. "Fine." Then he handed the phone to Leslie, oddly silent.

Hesitating for only a second, she brought the phone to her ear. "Uncle Hayden?" she asked, the buildup of terror seeping into her voice and making it break.

"Leslie?" Uncle Hayden let out her name like a long breath he'd been forced to hold for too long. "Leslie, please tell me you're okay."

"Yeah, I'm…I'm alive."

Uncle Hayden's words were rushed and serious—not like him at all—and worry made his voice higher than usual. "Leslie, you know I would do absolutely anything for you. You can trust me with anything. Do you know that?"

Whispers of tears welled in her eyes at his concern.

"Yeah," she mumbled, staring at the sidewalk. "I know."

"Okay, Les, this is very important. Just answer yes or no: are you in a situation that isn't safe?"

"Yes."

"Is Peter with people he shouldn't be?"

The question caught Leslie off guard. *He thinks this is about Peter?*

"Leslie," Uncle Hayden said sharply. "I understand if you're scared or don't want to get Peter in trouble, but I will not let his mistakes put you in danger. Do you understand me? If he dragged you into one of his situations, I will get you out, I swear. But you need to tell me what's going on."

Leslie glanced up at Peter who was watching her with earnest, as though through sheer concentration he could hear the whole conversation. She realized how easy it would be to throw him under bus. She could get herself out and safe with Hayden. He would help her with anything—she knew that. But as Peter's eyes bore into hers, nearly pleading, something in her chest broke at the thought of Bradley just walking into their secure house. Bradley would get to Hayden. Easy. And as much as Leslie wanted to be selfish, she'd never get over it if Hayden got hurt because of her.

"It's not Peter," Leslie breathed, and Peter let out long sigh of relief. "It has nothing to do with him. It's...something else. We have to get away from everyone for a while. It's not safe."

Uncle Hayden was pleading now, and she could hear the sound of his car revving to life in the background. "Leslie, please tell me what's going on. Please. I can help you. I will do anything for you. No matter what you've done or how far you think you're in. Please let me help you."

"I…" She shook her head and cleared her throat, willing herself to be strong. "I can't. It's not safe for you. Peter and I have to leave for a while. Just please tell our parents we'll be back. And not to go to the police. It's not safe."

"Les, I hear you, but please—"

"He'll hurt you, Hayden," Leslie whispered, cringing at the thought. "He'll hurt you and it will be my fault. So please just trust us. Trust me."

"I do, Les, I do. I really do. But who will hurt you? Let me—"

"I can't." Leslie took a breath to keep from breaking down. "Thanks Uncle Hayden. We'll see you soon." She bit the inside of her cheek as she pressed the end button, cutting off Uncle Hayden's pleas to help.

The silence was thick despite the bustle of Phoenix life around them. Peter let Leslie have space to compose herself before she went on with her plan.

Pulling up the browser on the phone, she searched the number she needed to call. It rang four times before a girl's voice came on.

"Ready Dawn Day Spa, this is Amanda. How can I help you?"

"Hi," Leslie started. "I need to set up an appointment."

"Um…what are you doing, Les—"

"Yes, my name is Lesa," she replied, too fast. "I need to set up an appointment. I have an emergency with…" She racked her brain for a moment to think what people even went to spas for. "With my eyebrows. It's an emergency."

"What are you doing?" Peter demanded. She waved him off.

112

"Uh yeah," Amanda said, finally catching up. "When would you like that appointment?"

"At ten," Leslie answered promptly. "With Rudy. Make sure they know it's an emergency."

"Got it. Ten with Rudy." Then Amanda pulled back her enthusiastic work voice. "We'll see you then! Thank you and have a great day."

Leslie hung up and handed the phone back to a confused Peter, who returned it to the giggling girls with thanks. She grabbed his arm and dragged him off before he could get carried away.

"Where are we going?" he asked, jerking his arm from hers as they walked.

"Back to Malquetta." She thought for a moment. "We're going to get three different cabs and go to three different ATMs. How much do you have in your accounts?"

Peter scoffed. "You think I know? I don't keep track of that stuff. Don't need to."

"Well, we will now."

"We can't just go home. That's where they think we'll go."

"We're not going home, pinhead. Trust me."

They got a cab that would drive them to their bank, where they withdrew as much money as the teller would let them. Then Leslie asked to go to a drive thru before getting dropped off seemingly in the middle of nowhere.

Peter shook his head as the cab left them in the dust, squinting through the sun that was starting to fall.

"So far, this is the dumbest idea you've ever had."

"You don't even know the plan, Peter." Leslie rolled her eyes and started walking down the deserted paved road, money stuffed in her pockets. "Chill."

"Where are we going?" he asked, keeping up with her.

"To Rudy."

"To what?"

"You'll see."

When the mini grove of trees began, Leslie turned right, heading into them and abandoning the road. The worn path was still there from all the years she'd used it. That brought a bit of comfort. Some normalcy.

It probably took fifteen minutes to get down the path—that's how long it usually took, if she remembered right—but it felt longer without a clock to check. Peter sighed melodramatically at least six times, but he never asked how far they were going. When they broke through the grove of trees, she stopped. Before her was a dirt parking lot people had made on a mountain ledge that overlooked the town of Malquetta, the lights from Phoenix still visible from miles away.

"This is Mt. Rudy," Leslie explained. "I know other people call it other things and use it, but we thought we discovered it in third grade, so we named it."

Peter actually laughed. "No, you didn't discover it. This is where Megan and I—"

"Nope." Leslie shook her head. "Don't wanna know that. Whatever you're gonna say. Don't need to know."

She backed up several yards into the safety of the trees before finding a rock to sit on. Peter sat on one next to her, and they started counting money.

"Nine thousand four hundred and twenty-seven dollars," Leslie finished, stacking up the hundreds of bills.

Peter stretched his legs out. "Yeah, I'm not worried. We'll be fine."

"I don't know. We can't just spend it all right out of the gate."

"I'm not stupid, Les. But we'll need stuff, like food and clothes and entertainment."

She shook her head. "It won't be like home."

"Why not?" Peter crowed. "We have almost ten thousand dollars. And we both still have a couple thousand we could flush out of the ATM when we need it."

Leslie folded up the wad of bills as best she could and went to put them in her pocket, but Peter grabbed her arm and motioned at her. With a sigh, she reluctantly handed the wad over. If he lost any of it, she'd kill him.

"We'll go to an ATM," Leslie thought out loud. "We'll go, like, fifty miles east of Malquetta—wherever that lands us—and withdraw there. Then we'll backtrack and head west."

"Why?" Peter snorted. "We'll lose miles."

"To throw Bradley off. He'll think he's following our trail." She let out a short breath and rubbed her arms even though she wasn't cold. "Besides, it's not like we're actually going anywhere."

Peter shrugged and folded his arms, trying not to show he was impressed and jealous she came up with the idea. "I guess."

They had to wait for hours. Leslie was restless, but she tried not to show it because Peter was way worse and she didn't want to be the hypocrite after yelling at him so much. Eventually the sun disappeared behind the mountains, but the air didn't seem to cool at all.

Several cars came, but Leslie didn't recognize any of them, so she stayed put.

Three cars had come and two gone when a loud revving ripped through the still night, accompanied by the roar of a motorcycle. Leslie stood, stretching out her stiff legs, so Peter stood too. That was their signal.

The blaring car seemed to choke as it was forced to the left, by the grove of trees, and skidded to a stop, the engine heaving before turning off. Amanda stepped out just as Chet pulled over on his motorcycle and parked. Then Amanda led the way to the grove of trees where Leslie and Peter stood waiting.

"You okay, Les?" Amanda asked before scowling when she saw Peter. "You didn't call emergency status 'cause of egghead Golden Boy, did you?"

Peter opened his mouth, but Leslie elbowed him in the ribs and spoke instead. "No, actually. It's…something else." She sighed. "But I'm not going to tell you."

Amanda pursed her lips, but Chet nodded solemnly. "We're here to help, Leslie. We don't need full disclosure to be your friend."

Leslie nodded, relaxing for the first time in what felt like days. "Okay, look, you can't tell anyone you saw us, okay? We called my parents and told them not to go to the police, but if we become 'missing kids' or whatever, then you didn't see us tonight. You have no idea what happened."

Both Amanda and Chet nodded in obedience, not surprised at all—emergency at Rudy was code for running away. But even in all their conversations and plans over the years, the three of them always assumed that if anyone actually had the guts to call emergency at Rudy, it would be Amanda.

"We're coming back," Peter added, almost unwillingly, still not wanting to admit he was talking to people he thought were beneath him. "A couple weeks tops. We just need to figure some things out."

Chet raised a thoughtful eyebrow, scrunching up the blue bandana around his forehead as he glanced at Peter. "Things that don't involve the police?"

Peter clenched his fists. "Look, dude, it's not my fault."

"Look, *dude*," Amanda spat, stepping in Peter's face and balling up her fists. "If you dragged Les into trouble, I'm gonna—"

"He didn't," Leslie said to get Amanda to back down. "For once, this isn't his fault. There's just a bad situation we got to avoid for a while. When it's blown over, we'll be back."

Amanda tossed something at Leslie—a key ring. "The tank is full and the trunk is stocked." She jerked her chin out at Peter. "As long as Golden Boy doesn't down it all in round one, you should have enough water, Red Bull, crackers, and jerky to last you a week. And we both donated old clothes that aren't too worn or old. Hopefully Golden Boy fits into something." She rolled her eyes. "Did you actually leave the letterman jacket at home?"

Peter gritted his teeth. "I don't have—"

"Stop," Leslie said, putting herself in between them and glancing at Peter. "We don't have time for this. He could already be out here looking for us."

"Ah," Amanda said with interest. "So, somebody's looking for you?"

Leslie shook her head. "Don't ask questions. Don't be interested. Don't do anything."

She tipped her head back and sighed. "Fine. I'll just have to pull a Nance and solve this mystery on my own."

"No, really," Peter said, a hint of fear in his voice. "This is bad news. Don't go poking around or…" He shuddered for a second and shook his head. "It's just a bad idea."

Amanda raised an eyebrow. "Wow, Golden Boy, you mean you actually care about something besides yourself?"

"I meant I don't want that on my head," Peter growled back. "Because you will get hurt."

"Amanda," Chet warned. Her eyes glinted with annoyance, but she backed off, her shoulders slumping as she resigned herself to staying in the dark.

Leslie rocked on her heels and twirled the key ring on her finger with a small grin. "Rudy's a go."

Amanda cracked a smile. "Ha, yeah. Guess it is. Who'd of thought."

"Be careful," Chet said, taking a step toward Leslie. "I trust you, Leslie, but the world won't."

"Oh brother," Peter muttered under his breath.

Then Amanda and Chet made their way over to his motorcycle. He forced her to put on a helmet he kept strapped to the back, then with parting nods, the bike roared to life, and they sped away into the night.

Peter held out his hand palm up. "Keys."

"Seriously?" Leslie scoffed. "Me and the two losers totally just saved your butt and that's all you can think to say?"

He didn't answer—he just took the key ring and sauntered to the beater, and Leslie trailed after. The car clanked to life. She tried not to think about the peeling leather seats that scratched against her arms as she secured her seatbelt across her body. After a few minutes of suffering through the deadly mix of Peter's driving and radio control, she noticed that one of her high tops had come untied. With the vehicle rattling underneath her, she brought her foot up and began the process of tying her shoe. It should've been simple. Easy. But without permission the rap music melted into Dad's voice.

Loop the ear, wrap it around, pull the other ear and whoop dee do, baby cakes, you've got a bunny rabbit. Now we better tie that little guy up. Wouldn't want to lose our rabbit, would we?

She took a shaky breath. *No, Dad, we wouldn't.* Then she put her foot back down and settled into the scratchy seat.

I want to go home.

Despite Leslie's doubts, the car got them twenty-five miles east. Peter wanted to just break into the Red Bull and keep going, but Leslie made him stop at a hotel so they could get some sleep. She waited in the car while Peter talked to the guy at the desk (making up some story about how their mom's reservation got lost—wrong, but effective) then they grabbed the duffel bag full of clothes and supplies from the trunk, and Peter led the way up the elevator and to room two thirty-five.

Leslie didn't think twice about staying in a big room with two beds and double bath and room service and flat screen TV, but when Peter emptied his pockets of money on the desk, she realized that someday they would run out. They couldn't live like this forever.

Peter laughed when he saw the pile of bills on the desk. "Look at all this! Now the real party can start."

Are you serious?

"Yeah, this'll be fun for three days and then it's going to get real." For some reason, her mind flashed to Naomi's scowl in the hospital, and the place she lived in. "You ready to go from six meals a day to two? Ready to live in trashy dumps and sleep on moldy floors and wrap up in musty sheets?" She clenched her fists. "We are freaking spoiled, Peter, and we don't even understand what life like this is going to be like."

"You're so freaking dramatic!" Peter exclaimed. "It's a few weeks, we have thousands of dollars, and we can do whatever we want."

"No, we can't! We're being hunted, Peter. Do you get that? Today was just day one, and if they really are looking for some key, Bradley will kill us to find it. We have to be crazy careful."

"So why don't we just find this key thing and turn it in?" Peter suggested. "Or just kill it. Whatever. Then it's over."

Leslie rubbed her forehead in frustration. He was giving her a headache. Like always. "You're so arrogant! Do you even understand our situation *at all*?"

"Don't pretend like you're so smart—you have no clue either. You just don't want to give me any satisfaction 'cause you're such a prick."

"No I'm not!" She stomped her foot. "You are *the* worst older brother in the history of awful older brothers. Ugh, I'd be so much better off on my own!"

Peter rolled his eyes. "Please, you wouldn't last five seconds."

"Five seconds longer than I would staying here. Wake up you conceited idiot—you're good for nothing." She sat down on the bed, crossing her arms tight across her chest, fuming. "Shouldn't have got my hopes up."

"That's BS," Peter muttered. "You've never thought anything better of me."

She laughed once but she didn't think it was very funny. "Oh yes I have. Since forever. No matter how awful or mean or just plain stupid you were, I always waited for you to be what I always thought you were. I waited for you to be amazing. To save my day. I knew you could. But you didn't." Her tone went edgy. "So I'm sorry I'm disappointed that when it really comes down to it—instead of being something better—you'll always just be you."

For once, her shouting rampage was met with silence. She watched her shoe, tense, waiting for the vicious comeback. It didn't come. That was weird; Peter was never quiet. A prickly feeling started coming over her, something totally foreign. What was that?

Then she realized: it was guilt. She felt guilty.

It was dumb she felt guilty. She didn't have to. She never had before. But despite her best efforts, she couldn't bring herself to lift her gaze from her shoe as the prickly feeling got worse with each second of passing silence.

She cleared her throat but couldn't get back the power her voice just had. "Just, uh…just pretend I didn't say that."

Silence.

She crossed her legs. "Really. I didn't mean it."

Peter drew in a breath, his voice quiet and tired like hers. "Yeah, you did."

"Didn't mean I had to say it."

"Well, you did."

"Pretend I didn't."

"Yeah." He sighed and headed for the bathroom. "Whatever."

The door shut behind him, and the shower started a few minutes later. Leslie puttered around the room for a while, counted the money again, then finally turned the TV on even though she didn't really watch it. When Peter finally came out an hour later, he crashed in the other bed without a word.

Leslie tossed and turned all night, sleeping in sporadic chunks because she was so tired, but never feeling rested. The insanity of the last few days played over and over in her head, making her mouth dry and fingers tingly, and she got up seven times throughout the night to check the locks on the doors and windows. It didn't help much. Nothing helped ease the all-consuming fear that was gnawing at her from the inside out. And even though she'd lashed out at Peter because of that fear, she had the feeling she was at least partly right: they weren't going home any time soon.

~~~

"Peter!" Leslie called as she sat on the edge of her bed and laced up her grey sneakers. "Are you getting close? We gotta go."

Dad's shoe-tying instructions filled her mind again as her fingers expertly tied the knots. She didn't shy away from the memory anymore—it'd been almost a year since she'd seen her parents, so she welcomed anything that would help her remember even the simplest things.
~~~

Loop the ear, wrap it around, pull the other ear and whoop dee do, baby cakes, you've got a bunny rabbit. Now we better tie that little guy up. Wouldn't want to lose our rabbit, would we?

The door to the bathroom opened and Peter stepped out, drying off his wet hair with a towel, then tossed it in the corner and pointed to his worn red t-shirt displaying a faded Arizona State logo.

"Check it out," he said with a grin. "Fitting, don't you think?"

Fitting, yes, since Peter should've been at college right now. He should've been starting his first semester at Arizona State, taking the football field by storm, while she should've been a few weeks into her senior year. That kind of life seemed so distant and unreachable—something she'd given up on hoping she'd have again. Life waited for no one. It always went on whether you were able to go with it or not.

Leslie laughed once, even though she only found it half funny. "It would've looked great on you."

Peter shrugged as he started gathering his stuff from around the dingy motel room and packing up the bed he'd made on the discolored floor. "Who needs college anyway?"

Not us, apparently.

She stood and helped him find everything: pocketknife, water bottles, first aid kit, two sets of extra clothes, three granola bars, and the few money bills they had left from their last raid. They'd been smart. Eventually. The first few months of their new situation were the worst of Leslie's life, easy. The whole last year had sucked, if she were honest, because living on the run from the ever-smarter Bradley Wheeler was an absolute nightmare. The world of infection turned out to be much bigger and more dangerous than Leslie had ever imagined. The hunt for the key was real and deadly, and both Peter and Leslie had suffered so much in the name of that hunt. They'd been run down, chased, found, kidnapped, and experimented on more times than Leslie had cared to count, Bradley bent on pushing every limit they had—physically, mentally, emotionally—just to see what made them break. And while Leslie used to consider herself a pretty put-together person, she now had more breaks and cracks and chinks than she could keep track of, and she was afraid for the day when she would just shatter into a million pieces and blow away in the wind. Lost. Forgotten.

Fear kept her going more than anything, except maybe obligation. Hope was scarce, but it would come back in fleeting breaths, and Leslie hung on to it when she could, knowing that inevitably it would disappear again. Peter had somehow managed to remain hopeful, or at least moderately confident, that things would work out eventually. His bursts of frustration, rage, or anxiety were volatile (and scary, if Leslie were honest) but usually only lasted the night. By the next morning, he was ready to go again.

Leslie had learned to rely on that. On Peter. Eventually, with much painful trial and error, they had learned to rely on each other. To run and hide and fight and live. They were on the same page now. It was easier to face the horrors Bradley brought when united with Peter, not against him.

The worn brown backpack they'd found at a thrift store six months back was filled and zipped up. Peter slung it over his shoulder, then took a deep breath and glanced at Leslie.

"You ready?"

She bit her lip and nodded. "Yeah." Rubbing her arms, she bounced a couple times on her feet, trying to pump herself up. She really didn't want an episode today. "Let's go."

But her voice fell flat as her lungs deflated, showcasing her anxiety. Peter nodded to himself, his expression serious but relaxed, and he put his hands on her shoulders.

"Just a few more hours," he told her, "and then we're free. When we go to sleep tonight, we'll be safe."

Safe. She couldn't remember the last time she'd felt safe. *Tonight, we're going to be safe.*

The thought made her insides both burst into ecstatic butterflies and constrict in nervous tension. She surged forward and gave Peter a giant hug.

"We'll be safe," she repeated with a small grin on her face. "That'll be nice."

Peter squeezed her back. "Yeah, it will." Then they broke apart, Peter put his dumpster sunglasses on, then opened the door to the outside world. Leslie's eyes did a quick sweep of the empty smelly motel room before she followed him out.

The sun was setting behind the mountains Leslie had grown up with, though the Rockies looked different here in Denver than in Malquetta. Maybe bigger. They were still there though, and that was comforting. Leslie glanced at them from time to time as she glanced everywhere else, matching Peter's ambling stride down the sidewalk.

Don't walk too fast. Not too slow. Give your steps purpose but not desperation. She reminded herself of the rules she and Peter had come up with—the best ways to avoid capture. And they really *really* needed to avoid capture today.

She watched the people they passed with mild interest. It had taken about four months of life on the run for the fear she felt toward the human population to dissipate. She didn't get afraid to pass people anymore. Sure, her body was still small, thin and rather weak looking—the infection formula didn't change her much in the way of appearance—but she could throw a punch now. A dang good one too, Peter told her.

The fear of the public was gone since she knew she could protect herself. The distrust wasn't.

Her steps were almost synchronized with Peter's as they made their way through Denver, passing by couples and families out enjoying the fresh August air, not stopping until they arrived at the location they were given: a park. As specified in the instructions, they sat in the third bench from the south end, right across from the playground. Then Peter reached underneath and found a package stuck to the bench, grabbing out the cellphone inside. The screen lit up when Peter pressed the home button, and he went into the contacts and called the only number saved.

Leslie leaned closer so she could hear the conversation too—this was something she didn't want to miss out on.

The phone rang three times before a young male voice answered. "Password, please."

Peter cleared his throat, and Leslie hoped he hadn't forgotten what he'd memorized. "Alpha, Delta, sixty-seven, forty-five, Maeser."

The voice broke out of grave seriousness into warm seriousness. "That's correct. Welcome aboard. I'm really excited to have you. It's Peter, right?"

"Yeah."

"And there's someone with you, right? The report I got says two."

"Yeah, it's me and my sister Leslie."

"Peter and Leslie," the guy repeated. Leslie couldn't help but smile at the friendliness in his tone. They needed some friends. "All right, awesome. I'm Brennan—I'm in charge of coordinating people to the club. I just gotta go through a few more questions before we can get the ball rolling. Are there any immediate threats?"

Leslie sensed Peter survey the park again before answering. "Not that we can tell."

"Good," Brennan responded in approval. "Any substantial injuries? We'll have a medical team on standby regardless, but it's good to know."

"No. We're fine."

"Awesome." It seemed like he was going through a checklist. "Name of your handler? I'm assuming you guys have the same one."

Leslie heard Peter's teeth snap together when his jaw clenched with hatred. "Bradley Wheeler."

"When was the last time you saw him?"

"Three days ago."

"Has he gone lethal?"

"That's what's crazy—he didn't used to. Just would lock us up and try all sorts of experiments on us. But about three months ago he started trying to actually kill us."

Brennan's voice somehow got nicer: not necessarily sympathetic but almost. "That's normal, unfortunately. His boss, Alexis, filed an extermination order. He wants us all dead." Leslie thought of the man with the wavy hair and eyes made of black holes—Alexis—and shuddered as Brennan took a breath. "But that's why we're here, right?"

"Isn't it because of the key?" Peter asked with a new kind of interest. Both Peter and Leslie had kept their eyes and ears out for the key during the time they'd been running from Bradley. Peter thought they could use it as some form of bargaining. "They accidently killed the rat and now they're wiping out the rest of us."

Brennan's warm friendly tone closed up, tight and vacuum sealed. "There's a lot of moving parts to this—a ton of things in play. Blaming people isn't what we're going for."

Peter scoffed, but Leslie elbowed him so he'd let it go. Not everyone had to agree with his utter disdain for the monster they'd never met. And she wanted Brennan to like them.

"So, what comes next?" Peter asked. "I take it we can't just walk right into your super-secret infected hideout?"

"No," Brennan answered, the full warmth to his voice not completely coming back. "Sorry. We run out of a nightclub that's been shut down. I'm the coordinator here, but my buddy Tristan will be the one that actually brings you in. It sounds like it will be a clean recruitment, so you should be fine with just him. He's great." Then he gave instructions to be back at the park bench in two hours with a new password to give Tristan, so he knew it was them, and asked for a quick physical description.

"Well, Peter," Brennan concluded, wrapping up, "we're excited for you to join our community. Best of luck—we'll see you tonight. Be safe."

"Yeah, you too," Peter said before hanging up.

Leslie straightened up and stretched her arms, her back aching from leaning at an odd angle against the bench for so long. "So, two hours, huh?"

Peter nodded as he twirled the phone around in his hand. "Yep. Kinda sucks. It's gonna be the longest two hours ever."

She nodded. "Pretty much."

They sat in silence for a moment, watching the people around them, parents calling warnings to their playing children that it was almost time to go. She smiled to herself when she saw a little boy triumphantly climb to the top of the highest slide and pump his fists.

"Remember when you pushed me down the slide and one of my teeth got knocked out?" Leslie asked.

Peter grinned and shook his head. "Hey, I was seven." He paused before muttering, "And I was trying to save the world from aliens."

She burst out laughing, and he tried to push her off the bench, but she braced her arm and caught herself with a victorious grin.

"You're so stupid, Les," Peter said, smiling, as he stood and gestured to the restaurant across the street. "You hungry? I get the feeling this'll be our last meal in freedom for a long time."

"Yeah, probably." Leslie stood and they started walking for the restaurant. "This infected club sounds like a summer camp and a prison had a weird baby."

He nodded. "Yeah, but it'll be safe. I think we both could use some boring."

"Boring sounds great."

The restaurant ended up being a burger joint, much to Peter's pleasure. It was almost eight thirty, so the place was pretty much empty besides a group of guys, one family, and two teenagers. Out of habit, Peter and Leslie headed for the corner booth without waiting to be seated—she let him sit on the one side so he could see the TV since there was some kind of game on. He watched the TV; she watched the front doors, absentmindedly flipping through the menu on the table. Waiting for Bradley to show up was life now. She felt like even when she was sleeping, she was waiting for him. Waiting for pain.

The waitress came over, interrupting her pondering, and Peter broke his concentration away from the TV to smile at her. Anna. Her nametag said Anna.

"Now what brings the two of you in here tonight?" she asked, setting down two water glasses, then pulling out her notepad and pen.

"Just grabbing a late dinner with my sister," Peter answered with way more animation than usual.

Leslie held back a groan. *Way to sneak that information in there. Subtle.*

Anna beamed. "That's great! What can I get you?"

"Let's see." Peter rubbed his hands together, glancing at his menu for the first time. "This is kind of a celebration, so we're gonna go big. I'll take your double decker cheeseburger with extra cheese—

actually make that extra everything. Large fries and, uh, large double fudge marshmallow brownie shake." He paused and gave Leslie a quick look before turning back to Anna. "Make that two shakes."

"You got it." Anna looked to Leslie. "Anything for you?"

She closed her menu, eyes still darting toward the front door. "I'll have the original burger and fries. No pickles though."

Anna scribbled onto her notebook with her nose scrunched in concentration. "All righty, anything else I can get for you guys?"

Peter shook his head, still smiling. "Nope, think that's it."

"Well then." She put her pen back in her apron pocket and gave Peter another grin. "I'll get that started."

Leslie waited until she was out of earshot before speaking. "You have no chance with her."

He took a drink of water and adjusted his focus back to the TV. "Oh, I think I do."

The family packed up and left the restaurant, a little girl proudly helping her mom clean up their table. Now it was just the group of guys and the couple left. She didn't recognize any of them, but that didn't stop her from continually checking up on their status.

We're going to be safe, she told herself. *In just a few hours, we'll be in a community with a bunch of other infecteds who get it, and we'll be safe.*

She wondered what that would be like: living with a bunch of other infecteds. It sounded absolutely fantastic, but she didn't want to get her hopes up too high, since everything in her life had crashed and burned. But to have friends again? Someone to talk to besides Peter? Someone else who might understand what horrible things she and her brother had been through? Now that would be awesome. They'd run into over a dozen infecteds over the months, making invaluable connections and learning more than they ever could've on their own, which is how they heard about the safe haven infected community. It was supposed to be great. She hoped it would be. She loved Peter and all, and she knew they'd be a team until the end, but they both needed other humans to interact with.

Yeah, even after nearly seventeen years of thinking Peter was completely and totally unlovable, Leslie realized one day months ago that she actually did. She had learned to. One of the many nights she couldn't sleep, she thought everything over, trying to decide the moment when she figured out how to love her idiot brother: it was the first time she heard him scream in pain. She didn't even know Peter could scream.

"Here you are," Anna said, appearing out of nowhere and making Leslie jump. "One original burger, one double decker cheeseburger—extra everything—two fries, and two shakes." She named the items as she set them on the table, then looked at Peter. "Anything else I can get you?"

He smiled back at her. "No, I think we're good."

"Well, you let me know, okay?" Either she had a weird twitch or she actually winked at Peter before leaving them to eat.

"Told ya," Peter said before digging into his monster burger.

"Barf," Leslie muttered as she picked through her fries. She ate one. It was salty—almost too salty. She took a drink of water to help. Another drink. That was it. She watched the door again, using her fingers to pick up a fry, hold it for a moment, then put it back in the basket, so it looked like she was doing something.

About ten minutes later, Peter broke her concentration. "Hey." Her eyes left the front door and met his, just as he gestured to her cooling food and melting shake. "No, we're not doing this. You eat."

Leslie sighed, trying to act innocent. "I did."

"I'm not blind, Les." Peter rolled his eyes. "You've had, like, two fries and that's it."

She scooted her basket away and wiped her fingers on a napkin. "I'm just not that hungry right now."

He checked the time on the phone they'd used to call Brennan. "The last thing you ate was at seven thirty this morning."

"I know, I'm just not—"

"It's been over twelve hours."

"I don't want it, Peter." She tried to divert the subject slightly, straightening her shoulders in resolve. "You can have it. You eat enough for two anyway."

He shook his head. "No way." Then he stood out of the booth and gestured for her to stand up. "Come on."

Automatically obeying, ready to run away from a threat she missed, she was surprised when he sat her in the opposite side of the booth, then took her spot.

Peter met her eyes resolutely, his tone firm but not mean, as he pushed her food to her. "You eat. I'll watch the door now."

"I don't need—"

"I'm not doing that again, Les," he cut in, a different edge to his voice. "I'm not. So eat, okay?"

That edge to his voice made Leslie fold. She nodded, then dropped her eyes and started nibbling on the edge of a fry. He rarely ever talked like that. The edge to his voice—raw desperation—only came out a few times. One of them was when she stopped eating. She just stopped one day, about three months into their new life on the run. Peter didn't notice. He didn't notice she always said 'no thanks' to food and was so tired and got so thin you could see all her bones.

Then one day she didn't wake up. Passed out and didn't wake up. Couldn't. Even with all Bradley had put her through, that was the second of three times she'd actually come close to dying. Peter had to take her to a hospital, then sneak her out before anyone discovered their IDs were fake and they were actually the missing Wyman kids. Shaking her awake—that was one of the select few times he had that desperate edge to his voice. Ever since then, he was a drill sergeant about her eating habits.

It took her an hour to eat everything. Peter went back and forth between watching the door and watching her, clearing his throat loudly when it had been a few minutes since she put something in her mouth. Anna came back over several times, but her beaming smile dimmed with each visit, as Peter gave all his attention to what Leslie was doing with her food. Once she was over halfway, he started eating his own stuff again, then eventually helped with hers when his was gone.

"See?" Peter said as she took the last sip of her soupy shake. "Not so bad, right?"

Leslie shook her head, then met his eyes evenly, her tone soft with gratitude. "No. It wasn't."

He nodded in approval before checking the time. "We still got, like, a half hour."

"Then let's just stay in here," Leslie said. "It's open for another hour, right?"

The less we're seen, the better.

"Fine by me." Peter stretched his arms and leaned back against the booth. "What do you think it's going to be like?"

"The hideout?"

"Yeah."

"I don't know." She swirled her water with her straw. "It almost seems too good to be true."

Peter nodded. "But it's there. We know it's real now. Sounds like a pretty strict place, but that's probably for the better. Less chance for mistakes."

"Yeah, probably."

Peter thought for a moment, hesitating, then tried to make his question seem like an afterthought. "You don't think they'll split us up, do you?"

She dropped her straw in her cup. She hadn't considered that. "Why would they do that?" she demanded hastily. "We're siblings. They can't."

He shrugged, failing at pretending like it didn't matter. "I don't know. Maybe they separate the guys from the girls."

Leslie shook her head at least three times. "I won't be okay with that."

"Good." Peter nodded again in approval, relaxing slightly. "I won't either."

They speculated for a while, debating on how warm the beds would be or what hobbies they'd pick up in their new free time or if any of the people they'd met would be there or if they were dead already. All too soon, it seemed, it was time to pay Anna and leave the safety of the restaurant to venture out to their new home.

It was cooler outside now, with the sun gone. Leslie hated the nighttime. In theory, she should like it, the shadows allowing her to hide better, but it was the opposite. The darkness made it harder for her to see, and that was way worse. She'd rather be out during the day: she could see everyone just as they could see her. An even playing field.

The streetlamps lit their way down the empty sidewalk and across the road to the park again. There were six or seven rowdy teenagers taking up the playground, shouting and laughing at what seemed like nothing, but that was it, besides the sporadic cars that went by. Leslie tried to match Peter's longer stride as they made their way to the third park bench. He was walking faster than usual.

He's nervous too.

The bench seemed harder than she remembered it. They both sat. She gritted her teeth at the obnoxious laughter echoing from the teenagers at the playground. Peter checked the time on the phone. It was eleven oh-one. He let out an impatient sigh through his teeth. Leslie was about to ask if it was too soon to be worried when the phone started ringing.

Peter answered it in a second. "Yeah?"

Leslie leaned closer to listen, right as an unfamiliar male voice responded, deeper than Brennan's. "Password please."

"May sixth two thousand and thirteen."

"Yep, that's correct." Then there was silence.

Peter checked the screen—the guy had hung up on them. He opened his mouth, probably to say something mean, but the same voice spoke up from behind them.

"You ready?"

Both Leslie and Peter jumped and turned to find a guy standing there: probably Leslie's age, an inch shorter than Peter though he held himself with a posture of capability, making him seem tougher. Streetlamp light glinted off the shark tooth that hung on a string around his neck.

"Peter and Leslie?" he asked, his murky brown eyes calculating.

Peter nodded. "Yeah."

"Good. I'm Tristan." He shook both of their hands. "Nice to have you." His eyes took in both of them before stopping on Leslie. "You ready to go?"

She nodded, the thought of finding a home warming her up from the inside out.

We're going to be safe.

"All right, good. Here's the deal: you're both going to have to trust me. It looks like it'll be a quiet night, but regardless, you need to know I have your back. Got it?"

Leslie and Peter nodded. Whatever it took.

Tristan gestured to the street behind them. "Okay, we're about six blocks over. We'll head in the back way though. Follow me."

They took seven steps before Leslie skidded to a stop and sucked in a sharp breath. Peter noticed and stopped too, causing Tristan to turn and see what the problem was. But Leslie wasn't paying attention to them. She was watching the empty playground.

Peter automatically reached over and wrapped his arm around her shoulders, letting her use his solid frame as support, like he did whenever she had an episode. But for once, that wasn't it.

"What's wrong?" Tristan asked, his tone not quite impatient, but rushed.

Peter's voice had a slight air of defensiveness. "She just needs a minute sometimes."

Leslie shook her head. "No, that's not it." She pointed to the playground, now devoid of obnoxious teenagers. "Look."

The boys followed her finger. Tristan shrugged. "I don't get it."

"They're gone," she explained, her voice hollow. "He's here."

"How do you know?" Tristan demanded.

Peter's hold on her shoulders changed from supportive to protective, his head moving back and forth as he surveyed the now empty park. "She just does. She's always right."

Tristan motioned for them to follow, waiting until they were under a giant tree before stopping and whipping out a phone. The screen glowed in the darkness, and Leslie squinted when he turned it to them. On the screen was a picture of Bradley, head on, like on a driver's license.

"This is him, right?" Tristan asked.

Leslie took a deep breath and nodded. That was him.

"How'd you get that picture?" Peter asked. "You got someone on the inside?"

Tristan pressed his mouth into a thin line, hesitating. "Yeah, something like that." He put his phone away, trading it for a handgun. "We're going to get you there safely. Stay on my back and stay alert. We'll have to take another route, a longer one, just to be safe—we cannot under any circumstances expose the club. Do you both understand me?"

"Yes," they answered at the same time.

Tristan pressed something on his phone and brought it to his ear, looking behind his shoulder before speaking, voice low and hasty.

"We got a problem. They think their handler's here. I haven't seen anything, but they're confident." He glanced at them, then quickly looked away. "Please tell me *he's* there. And sober."

Who's he? Leslie wondered. *They're keeping secrets from us already?*

Whoever 'he' was must've been unavailable, because after listening a moment, Tristan sighed. "Figures. What does Alaina think?" More listening. "My thought will always be better safe than sorry." More listening. "But Alaina shouldn't be out anyway—we all know Lennon has a million-dollar reward on that red head. I…Fine. Desperate times, I guess. Yeah." He hung up and put the phone is his back in his pocket.

Peter shifted his weight, his arm still around Leslie. "So what do we do?"

Tristan nodded his head in the direction of what must've been the club. "Brennan and Alaina are on standby if we need them, but we have to try and do this on our own. If too many of us appear in the same area, someone's gonna find us out." He gestured for them to follow. "We'll just be careful. You know your guy best. Let me know if you notice the slightest thing." He nodded at the playground. "Besides the empty park."

Peter made Leslie go ahead of him so she was sandwiched in between the two boys as they darted through the trees. Eventually, though, they ran out of trees. They had to go out in the open. Tristan kept his gun hidden in his jacket, his shaggy brown hair lifting in the slight breeze. The brown of his hair matched the brown of the closed clothing store they passed. A mannequin in the window had a blue gown on, the deep dark blue that matched the color of the starless sky. It also matched the color of the car parked in the parking lot a street over.

The car was off. It wasn't the only car parked in the lot, but it caught Leslie's attention because of the giant scuffed scratch on the front right corner.

"It's Jasper," she hissed through her teeth.

Tristan didn't turn when he asked, "Who?" just as Peter growled, "Where?"

"Bradley's assistant." She kept her head forward too, barely moving her mouth. "To the left, across the street, third car from the right."

"Is he in it?" Tristan asked.

She glanced sideways, keeping her head straight forward. "Can't tell."

"So he's hiding."

"No," Peter muttered, nearly shaking with hatred. "He's calling us out."

"He wants us to know they're here," Leslie agreed.

Once the parking lot was behind them, she heard a car start and tires munch against tiny gravel. Her heart started beating twice as fast.

Tristan heard it too; she saw the muscles in his shoulders tighten. Again, he didn't turn his head when he spoke, his soft voice strained. "If you split up, who would they follow?"

"Bradley would go after Peter," Leslie answered.

Peter clenched his teeth. "Jasper would follow her."

"Can you shake them?" Tristan asked.

Peter shrugged. "We have before. But we haven't before too."

"You think we should split up?" Leslie guessed. She didn't want to, but it had worked in the past, and with Tristan as backup, they might be able to pull it off.

"It's an idea. Break off as three, cripple them separately if needed, then meet back up and disappear."

The road in front of them grew brighter as the car behind them grew closer. They had to decide right now.

"Half a block down," Leslie ordered. "Third alley in, duck and we'll go."

Tristan gave a curt nod. Peter realized he was taking too big of steps and slowed down slightly, so they were in more of a line. Leslie forced her eyes to stay forward, keeping her head from turning to look behind, watching as the grey of the cement went under them and the browns of the buildings went past. The car didn't go by. It was crawling behind them. Leslie somehow kept herself from shivering—it was Jasper.

We're going to be safe. Just get through this, and you can sleep. Actually sleep, soundly. Safely. It was worth the risk for that.

The first alley went by. They stayed strong. The second. Third was coming. The second the corner came, Peter jerked around it, and they followed him, dashing down the narrow alley and breaking through on the other side, a different road, hearing the screeching of brakes in the distance.

Tristan pointed across the street as they ran. "Two streets down, three blocks over, next to a physical

therapy office. Meet me there as soon as you're safe."
Then he went left.

Peter started to go right, so Leslie ran straight for two steps until he grabbed her arm and jerked her to a stop.

"Where are you going?" he demanded.

She nodded her head to the left, impatient.

"Splitting up. Did you not hear what we just said?"

He shook his head. "Not you. You can't go by yourself. Not tonight."

"Why?" She tried to yank her arm out of his grip, kind of annoyed with his doubts. "I'll be fine."

But he wasn't convinced, rocking on his heels, as the desperation started to creep into his eyes and voice.

"Les—"

"We'll be safe, Peter." She tried to calm him with her hopeful gaze. "Safe. Finally."

She could tell he saw the vision too, the sensation of safety they were so close to tasting. His face got serious and resolute, then he gave a curt nod before taking off in his direction, and she bolted the second he let her go.

Thankfully, there were no cars to hit her when she scurried across the street, the asphalt firm under her feet. She knew going in a straight line was a bad idea—it was best to zigzag as much as possible, especially where a car couldn't follow. So she went through another alley and broke out on the other side, then veered left. And again. Across the street. Down the alley. Nobody was following her, at least that she could tell. She went a street farther than she was supposed to, and a block too far, not wanting to reach the meet up spot until she was completely sure she'd lost Jasper.

Wanting to break and regroup, Leslie ducked behind a movie theater, catching the aroma of fresh popcorn and warm butter as she crouched in between two of the four dumpsters. Breathe in. Breathe out. She felt her chest rise and fall as she reminded herself to pause. Overexerting was always a bad idea. Even when living on the run, she found she needed to force herself to stop every once in a while. Just stop amid the storm of stress and breathe. It helped her focus and be more effective in the long run.

After several good deep breaths, she listened. One car passed by. Then another. Normal speed. No crawling cars filled with creeps or murderers.

This could actually work. We're going to be safe.

She gave a quick thought to Peter, but only a quick one—they'd both learned to not worry about the other. Or, at least, try very hard not to. Worry was a distraction that often turned nearly lethal. They knew how to take care of themselves, separate or together. And that Tristan kid seemed like he knew what he was doing. Plus, he had a gun.

This is so going to work.

The quiet, still seconds turned to minutes as she waited. Listened. Breathed. She was in the clear; she knew it. Her leg muscles whined as she started to bring herself up from her crouch, prepared to go meet up with Tristan and Peter. Then she heard shoes scraping against bits of gravel, and quickly sunk back down.

Keep your head, Leslie. That's what Peter would say when she was about to freak out in a sensitive moment. *Keep your head. Stay calm.*

Then the footsteps stopped. Where was he? And *who* was it? It was probably too much to hope that it was Peter looking for her.

Another car went by but that was the only sound Leslie's straining ears could find. Then he spoke, his voice low and glossy, but slimy too. Like a snake. Like a thin little snake you didn't think was dangerous until it lunged out and bit you with poisonous fangs.

"Come on out, little Leslie. I know you're around here." The footsteps started again and Jasper's voice got closer. "There's no point in hiding. Come on out."

She waited, holding her breath, heart hammering in her chest. He was going to find her. She knew that. Better take any advantage she could possibly get.

Jasper kept walking, steps slow and meticulous, down the alley, waiting for her to poke out. Leslie saw the shadow of his thin frame pass by her spot, his ashen hair sticking out in every direction like he'd been electrocuted, then hesitate. He would check between all the dumpsters. He'd find her.

Keep your head, Leslie. Keep your head. We're gonna be safe.

The shadow bent toward the dumpster next to her, and she jumped up, lurching out of her hiding spot. Whipping around, she landed a powerful kick in the center of his back. He fell forward to his knees, and she kicked him again, forcing him all the way to the ground. Then she hit her foot against his head to effectively smash it against the cement, and took off.

She got three steps before he snatched her ankle and yanked her down to the ground too, grimacing when she landed on her shoulder. He crawled forward to get a good vantage point over her, so she threw out her elbow—ramming it into his nose—and kneed him in the gut, making him grunt in pain and fall over.

Before she could get all the way back up, though, he had her again. They rolled around on the ground for a lasting minute, throwing punch after punch and elbow after elbow. Her elbows were Leslie's weapons of choice. The fight was hazardously close, but her elbows saved the day: she nailed him right in the mouth and he doubled over spitting. Blood. Something white. A tooth.

Using the distraction, she jumped up and grabbed his atrocious hair, something he always did to her, then slammed his head against the dumpster with all the force she had. Boom. Again. And again. He was down, but his finger twitched, so she hit his head one more time. His body went limp on the ground, and she couldn't help but grin at the sight.

Nailed it.

Crouching down again, she nudged his jacket with her foot until she found the holster for his handgun and slid the weapon out. It was heavier than she thought it would be. She tested the weight of it in her hands for a moment before wiping some blood off her face with the back of her hand and standing up. One down. Bradley to go.

Peter could take him though. Leslie knew that. With the stakes this high, even if Bradley cornered him in an alley, Peter could take him on and squash him.

Keep your head, Peter. We can do this.

Taking a deep breath, she went to stow the stolen gun under her shirt and head for the meet up spot. About fifteen feet ahead, a figure slid into the alley, blocking her path. She relaxed at the thought of Peter, but froze when she saw it was Bradley.

"Leslie," he greeted, a stupid grin on his face to match the airheaded tone he always used. His ego hadn't diminished over the months. "Nice night, huh?"

Keep your head, Leslie. She could hear Peter's voice in her mind. *Stay calm. It's gonna be fine.*

Curling both hands around Jasper's gun, she raised her arms and aimed the barrel right at Bradley. His eyebrows shot up as he slowly raised his hands, one of them holding his cell phone, and he glanced around her to see Jasper's unconscious body. His eyes widened in understanding. And caution. He knew she'd use the gun if she had to. She had before.

"I'd think twice about that," Bradley said, nodding at her weapon.

She made sure her voice was even. "I'm leaving." Keeping her eyes and weapon on Bradley, she took a step backwards. Then another. He wasn't going to get her. Not this time. Not tonight.

We're gonna be safe.

"I've got Peter." He said the sentence in passing, like it was no big deal, the slightest air of taunting to his words.

Her footsteps halted, but she stopped her mind from going there. Bradley was a proven liar on that subject. She'd need evidence.

"Right," she said, her tone derisive, but she couldn't bring herself to keep retreating. "I've heard that one before."

In the darkness, she could barely see the shadow of his thumb as it moved. His phone glowed to life in his hand, illuminating his maniacal smile. Then he pressed the phone screen again. Peter's scream of agony ripped from the phone speakers, tearing apart the stillness of the night.

Leslie's stance faltered. Her breathing caught and her chest seemed to cave in, her shoulders hunching over and legs shaking.

"Stop," she whispered, her voice breaking. She recoiled at the excruciating sounds. "Stop!" Finally gaining volume, she stepped forward, desperate. "Call them off, Bradley! Stop it now!" Her arms fell, the gun at her side, as she continued surging forward, the horrors drawing her in like a magnet. "Please! Leave him alone!" She couldn't take another second. She couldn't.

Bradley's arms shifted, like he was going to grant her wish and speak orders to release in the phone, but at the last second, he reached out of sight with his other hand. Mercifully, the screaming stopped, a muffled cracking sound taking its place.

The impact bore into Leslie. She dropped her gun. It clattered on the cement. She staggered forward, then her knees gave out—Bradley rushed over and caught her on the way down, pressing his gun into her side. Another cracking sound. Leslie's body recoiled from the pain. Her shirt felt wet. She glanced down to find a growing red spot on her stomach.

"Shh," Bradley whispered in response to her gurgled gasping. "Shh, little Leslie. You'll see Peter again soon enough."

More cracking sounds, from farther away. Bradley lost his grip and Leslie fell onto the ground. She couldn't breathe. She clutched her wet stomach, thinking somehow that would stop the overwhelming anguish that emanated from it. She heard scuffling. Cracking. What was that?

Then arms around her. She focused her eyes just as Peter leaned over her. His face was…scared. Peter was scared about something.

He pressed his hands over hers, both of them soaking in red. "Why'd you drop it, Les?" he demanded, his voice hoarse with panic. "You had him. You…" He looked over her again, eyes wide. "Why'd you do that?"

She couldn't find enough air. Gasping. Something was clogging her throat. "He…he tricked…me," she managed to get out. "He…had…you…and…"

Then Tristan was there, standing over both of them, his calm composure gone but still in control.

"We gotta go now!"

Peter nodded and scooped Leslie up in his arms. She cried out at the jostling. The night sky started blurring. She kept her hands on her stomach. They were warm and wet and sticky.

"Hurts," she whispered. "Hurts."

Stop the hurt, Peter. Please make it stop.

Then the night sky was gone. The air changed: stuffier. Even harder to breathe. It got louder, the buzz of frenzied yelling filling her ears. Peter set her down on something hard, made sure she was stable, then held her face in his sticky red hands.

"Stay with me, Les," he told her, his voice somehow firm and fragile at the same time. "You stay with me, okay?"

"Hurts," she whimpered. "Hurts."

"I know." He brushed her hair out of her face. "I know, Les. I know. Just stay with me. You have to stay with me."

Peter was pushed to the side then, one boy and one girl—both blondes—taking over, shouting orders at the other strangers frantically bustling around her. A girl with brilliant crimson hair shot some liquid into Leslie's arm; she was alarmed when she found she couldn't feel it.

I'm dying, she realized. *I'm dying right now.*

148

"She needs blood," the blonde girl said, her bare arms covered in red up to her elbows. "Now."

"Take mine," Peter ordered, stepping forward. The blonde girl glanced at him with hesitation, making his frustrations boil over. "We're a match, I know, just take it!"

Leslie felt heavy. Weighed down. Her heart felt like it was going faster than humanly possible, and she knew it was about to give out.

"Peter," she whispered, liquid dripping out of her mouth and down her face. He was there in an instant, bringing his face closer to hers so that's all she could see.

"Les, you gotta hang in there, okay?" There was that desperate edge again, like when she'd nearly starved to death. "Les, please. They're giving you blood; you're gonna be fine. You just gotta stay with me."

But she was starting to see black spots. Peter was fading from her, his voice getting quieter, his presence getting farther and farther away.

"Pet—Peter." She struggled with the words, her body not responding to her sluggish mind the way it should. But she had to get this out. Before it was too late.

"Yeah, Les." He sounded oceans away. "What? Les?"

"Tell…tell Mom. Tell her…her…I'm…sorry… okay?"

His eyebrows creased, sending fault lines through his face as though he were breaking. "No, Les. Don't talk like that. You tell her. You gotta…" He took a deep breath. "You have to stay with me. Please. Please, Les, you have to. Don't leave me here."

She closed her eyes. They wouldn't stay open. "Peter." Her shoulders relaxed. Her heart went from sprinting to crawling. Struggling to beat. She could barely feel the tongue in her mouth. The room seemed to shrink but the atmosphere had grown. Bigger. Lighter. She felt she was floating. "I…I…love. Love. You."

"Les? Les? Can you hear me? Les!"

Leslie wanted so badly to open her eyes, to talk to him, let him know everything was going to be okay. But she couldn't. The world had faded. She was gone.

Keep your head, Peter. You're gonna be all right.

Emilee King is the author of the Arie's Story survival series and the Elarian Chronicles. She loves fairy tales, superheroes, fantasy, and murder mysteries, and is constantly on the hunt for good stories. When she's not writing, you can find her reorganizing her bookshelves, eating pasta, beating the high score on Galaga, or spending time with her family. Visit her website at emileeking.com